To Mari

love Miriane

THE LITTLE DANCER

Books in the series

DANCING PEEL
DANCER'S LUCK
THE LITTLE DANCER
DANCER IN THE WINGS

THE LITTLE DANCER

by

LORNA HILL

Illustrated by Anne Grahame Johnstone

AWARD PUBLICATIONS LIMITED

to
DAME FLORA
the Macleod of Macleod
Dunvegan Castle
Isle of Skye

ISBN 0-86163-840-9

First published 1956 by Thomas Nelson and Sons Ltd
This edition first published 1997

Published by Award Publications Limited,
27 Longford Street, London NW1 3DZ

Printed in India

CONTENTS

Part One

1 AUTUMN IN SKYE

Airdrochan Castle stood on a rocky headland on the northern shore of Loch Slapin, on the Island of Skye. The rugged building was connected to the island by a stony causeway, against which the waves dashed when the loch was rough, and drenched with spray anyone who happened to be walking along it. The setting sun glinted on its narrow windows, giving it a sinister appearance, and indeed so many murders, massacres, clan fights and dark deeds of all kinds had been perpetrated within its walls that the atmosphere of the past hung about it like a veil, tinging the very air with gloom. Yet it was beautiful, too, with a certain wild loveliness.

At the time of this story, however, the castle could not have been called sinister, for it had been rented to a family of rich Americans. Mamie Slaughter had covered its echoing stone passages with warm carpets and filled its vast cold rooms with many heaters in an attempt to 'warm it up a bit'. Deborah, the Slaughters' only daughter, was away at a Swiss finishing school, and this was the reason for her parents' prolonged stay in Europe, on the remote Scottish island. Deborah was seventeen, and was just like a full-blown, pink-petalled rose, with the dew still upon it. Her hair was pure gold, her skin milk and roses, and she smelled deliciously of French perfume. She was like a rose in other ways, too. Beautiful, candid, loving warmth and sunshine; there was no subtlety about Deborah Slaughter.

On the other hand, Jaimie Gordon, the laird of Airdrochnish, who owned the castle, was fashioned in another mould. All the mystery of the remote mountain fastnesses and the deep lochs of his island home was in Jaimie's dark eyes.

Due east of the castle, about a quarter of a mile away on the shore, white cottages could be seen clustered round a little bay of glistening white sand. This was Jaimie's village of Airdrochan and beyond it, to the north, half hidden behind a grove of silver birch trees, was the little cottage where Jaimie himself lived while the Slaughters occupied his castle. A haze of peat smoke hung in the soft autumn air, for it was October, one of the loveliest months in the Hebrides.

On a terrace in front of the castle sat Mamie Slaughter in a chaise-longue. She was writing a letter to her old friend Miriam in faraway Chicago:

I'm getting kinda fond of Skye, anyway it's fine for Pop. He's sure got something to interest him – fishing! Believe me, honey, there are more fish in Skye than in most other places, and they all come straight to Pop! Every day he and Murdo – he's the laird's gillie and an awful silent man – bring home a basket brim-full of fish. We have fish at every meal, and it's my idea we'll be growing fins soon, or tails, like mermaids! Maybe it's just as well, for goodness knows it's difficult enough to get meat in this place, especially now that the stream's washed away the road near Coirechatachain, and goodness knows when they'll get it mended. They sure don't hurry things in this old island! But as a matter of fact, between you and me and Pop's fish, it's quite convenient for us to stay on here until next autumn, when young Deb will have finished at Beau Rivage – that's the name of her Swiss school – and we'll be able to give her a 'Season' in London before we fly home.

Well, honey, I think I have told you most everything, so I will stop now. With all good wishes and love from your old friend,

Mamie.

She folded the sheets and pushed them into an airmail envelope, then helped herself to a candy out of a large box at her elbow. Yes, it was convenient all round, she thought, tucking a tartan rug round her knees. The laird himself was mighty glad of the generous rent paid him by the Slaughters for the use of his castle. He'd said so! To be sure, he would get well paid, by and by, for his work on the film they were making in the island – the film that was to be called *Pride o' the North*, but he hadn't got that money yet so the Slaughters' rent would just tide him over nicely. He had assured Mamie of this in his beautiful, dignified, slightly stilted English; had told her that they were very welcome to stay in his castle as long as they wished. For the present, all the filming was being done in the London studios, but later on, when the weather was set fair – which would be in May, Jaimie said – they would come to Airdrochan and other places in the island and film the real thing. When Mamie heard this, wild horses wouldn't have driven her home. To be living in an old Scottish castle while a film was being made there – what a story it would make back home! She'd have enough to talk about for years!

Meanwhile the weather remained fine, though during the night a feather of snow had appeared across Blaven's frowning brow. Blaven was the big, rugged giant of a mountain that rose from the rough moorland on the opposite shore of Loch Slapin. It wouldn't be long before winter was here. The brooding hills seemed to be waiting for something – waiting for the first snows of winter, thought Mamie with a shiver. She rose and went indoors, shouting for Morag to come and light a fire in the lounge.

'It gets awful cold at nights,' she said to herself. 'I'll have to get more heaters from some place in time for Christmas.'

With the curtains drawn and a cheerful log fire crackling in the huge open fireplace, Mamie sat down at her bureau and amused herself by writing out

menus for Christmas and the New Year. Deb would be here, and the laird, and of course herself and Pop. That would be four of them altogether. Then there was Sheena. She'd invite her too. Her heart ached for the poor child, living in that great old house at Glendounie, with only an invalid mother to keep her company. Young things needed young company, thought Mamie Slaughter. There were rumours going round Airdrochnish, the district round Airdrochan which composed Jaimie's estate, that Sheena's mother hadn't long to live, and that when she died, Jaimie Gordon would be made her guardian, together with her uncle, Malcolm MacCrimmon, who no longer lived in the island but was the vicar of a tiny parish in Northumberland in England. Heaven help the poor child, thought Mamie, with the laird for her guardian! It wouldn't surprise Mamie if, when the sad event occurred, the laird kept his young ward in mourning for a full six months! And of course what *he* said 'went', as Mamie put it. The laird was all-powerful. If he wanted to keep Sheena wearing black until she was twenty-one, in black she'd have to be!

Once Mamie had thought in her match-making heart that Jaimie and Sheena would hit it off together – the one so dark, the other tawny as a beech tree in the fall. But they didn't seem to show the least partiality for each other, at least not in Mamie's candid eyes. She imagined how a young American would greet his best girl after a prolonged absence. But Jaimie would just greet Sheena with his stiff little bow – almost as if she were a stranger. And Sheena would give him her hand coolly, self-possessedly. Mamie Slaughter was not sensitive, or she would have felt that these two were not quite so unaware of each other as they appeared. Jaimie's dark glance lingered for a moment on Sheena's shining hair, and the girl's long green eyes fell before his own.

If Mamie, and other people too, were puzzled by the common knowledge that the laird was to be Sheena's joint guardian, Jaimie, himself, was not. He knew exactly why Sheena's mother had made this provision in her will, for she had told him as she lay pale and weak in her great four-poster bed in the old house at Glendounie. But what she had said had been in strict secrecy, and Jaimie was not one to betray a confidence. What Caitriana MacDonald had said he kept locked in his heart.

It was on the following morning that Jaimie set out to walk to Camus Fhionnairidh, the Sheiling of the White Sands, which in the English is Camasunary. His car was, as so often happened, out of commission and, in any case, the place where he was going was so remote that a car would have been more of a liability than an asset. Having crossed Loch Slapin in his little rowing-boat, he drew it up on to the shingle and set off down the Kirkibost road. After a couple of miles he turned up a by-road leading to Strathaird House, and thence took a rough track up into the foothills of Blaven. At length he rounded the shoulder of the hill and an awe-inspiring sight met his view. He was looking up into a wild open corrie, and facing him were the precipices of the south-east face of Blaven. Now the path rose again to a ridge, from the top of which he could see below him the tiny white cottage which was the only dwelling at Camasunary.

He also saw Andrew MacKinnon, bucket in hand, moving from cottage to byre, and this told him that the sick cow he had come all these rough miles to visit was, at all events, still alive. Jaimie never thought of the long distances he had to travel – it was all in the day's work for a veterinary surgeon in this lonely island . . .

His visit at an end, he set off along the cliff-top for Elgol, where his next call was, and where he hoped to charter a motor-boat which would take him across to Glendounie, nestling in its woods behind Tarskavaig. To his right, over the blue waters of Loch Scavaig, marched the wild and jagged silhouette of the Black Cuillin, with the huge bulk of Blaven (the Blue Mountain) directly behind him. It was one of the loneliest and most beautiful walks in the whole island, and Jaimie stopped more than once not only to get his breath, for the going was rough in the extreme, but to admire the view. At the highest point of the path he stopped once more. Cradled in the midst of a ring of shattered peaks he could see a glint of the dark waters of Loch Coruisk. Jaimie stood for a long while drinking in the view, for he might not be walking over this path for a long time to come. Next month he was crossing over to the mainland on his way to London. There he would remain, working at the film studios on the picture that was to make his fortune. Not until April or May would he return, except for a couple of days at the New Year maybe, and then he hoped it would be for ever. The money he made with this one film would repair his castle and his estate and set him on his feet. With his simple needs he would be able to go on living here for the rest of his life, and leave his estate in good order to his next of kin. He had no use for the film making, and never intended to make another, but he felt that this one had been sent direct from heaven in answer to his prayer. He ran a sunburnt hand through his curly black hair and then bowed his head, remaining quite still for a few minutes, thanking God, who had indeed been good to him. He was, at this moment, supremely happy.

The sun was going down when he stepped from the motor-boat owned by Sandy MacFarlane on to the tiny jetty in Tarskavaig Bay. From here he took the road northwards and before very long came to the little village of Glendounie. It was very peaceful, but quite unlike the wild magnificence of the scenery on the far shore. Glendounie House was some way out of the village, and a bridle-path led to it, crossing a stream by a little stone bridge. The house stood at the foot of a craggy black hill which sheltered it from the cold northerly winds. To the south lay wide rough fields, and in their midst a blue lochan.

Inquiring at the house for the young mistress, for so she was known, he was told that she was away seeking mushrooms, which abound on the boggy soil of Skye.

'It is a long time since she is gone,' said Mairi Campbell, one of the two servants that remained to the impoverished house of the MacDonalds of Glendounie. 'It is time she was at home,' added Mairi, 'with the night falling and the *each dubh* coming up out of the loch.'

Jaimie's dark brows drew together. What the woman said was true. It was no time of night for a young girl to be out by herself. He believed implicitly in the existence of the evil water-horse that lived in the depths of the loch and came out at night, with seaweed dripping from his mane, to carry off young and beautiful maidens. After ascertaining that the old mistress was asleep, and giving strict orders that she must not be disturbed, he set off to look for Sheena, who was indeed both young and beautiful – fit prey for any prowling water-horse.

And so it was that he came upon her. She was perched high in the branches of the one tree of size the pasture contained and below her, bellowing in fury and trampling into the earth her basket of mushrooms, was not an *each dubh* but Black Diarmid the bull. As a rule Highland bulls are gentle enough and quite harmless, but Diarmid was in a bad temper. His pasture had been changed and he could no longer bellow in friendly fashion to the cows in the field across the way. He was lonely; he was sad. Moreover the sun had been hot and the flies had tormented him. And now, who should invade his domain but a detested human being. He had put down his shaggy head, pawed the ground and roared a warning. Sheena, thinking of other things, had ignored the warning, and had gone on picking mushrooms. So Diarmid had charged the intruder.

At the very moment when Jaimie arrived on the scene, the high branch on which Sheena was perched gave way and Sheena was thrown to the ground, with only the slender tree-trunk between her and the maddened bull. In a flash Jaimie acted. He must do something to distract the animal's attention. He ran forward towards the tree, shouting and waving his arms.

'Climb up again! Climb up again!' he yelled. 'Climb quickly!'

Diarmid looked round to see what the noise was and who or what the intruder might be, and in these few seconds Sheena was up in the tree again. It was certain that she could never have climbed it in cold blood, but now she did so, knowing that almost certain death awaited her if she failed.

Meanwhile Diarmid had turned his attention to Jaimie. He put his great head down and charged. Jaimie, instinctively using bullfighting tactics, tore off his plaid and held it to one side of his body, tempting the bull with it. A second later Diarmid thundered past, impaling the plaid on his horns and carrying it away with him. In an instant Jaimie was up in the tree with Sheena and there the two of them crouched, the young man astride a branch, the girl cowering in a fork of the trunk, while below them, only just out of reach, bellowed Diarmid, now and then making mad rushes at the tree and sending shivers through the trunk with the impact of his powerful body.

Suddenly Jaimie saw that Sheena had fainted and was slipping from her perch. He leaned forward perilously, nearly losing his own balance, caught her just in time to prevent her falling, and cradled her in his arms. There was nothing he could do to rouse her. He must just wait, holding her, until she came to her senses. Her red-gold head hung back against his shoulder and her face looked pathetically white. On a sudden instinct he drew her closer and kissed her tenderly, knowing that she would never know that he had done so.

After a few moments she came to herself with a sigh and a shiver, for now that the sun had set it was bitterly cold. On the ground, some distance away, lay Jaimie's plaid that would have kept them both warm, but for all the good it was it might just as well be in Australia, thought Jaimie with a twist of his lips.

The moon rose and flooded the pasture with a pale, unearthly light. The cold air drew out the heat in the ground and a slight mist rose. Below the tree the untiring Diarmid still snorted and trampled the peaty soil, while above in the forked branch clung Jaimie

and Sheena, the girl trembling with fright, the man wondering what he could do to drive away the infuriated bull.

And then, quite suddenly, Diarmid gave up the struggle. The cool night wind had driven away the flies, the pasture no longer looked strange to him in the moonlight. He forgot about the hated human beings in the tree, or lost interest in them. Before Jaimie and Sheena's unbelieving eyes he threw up his head and trotted briskly away towards the little fir-wood on the far side of the field, and began to graze the soft green grass that grew round the edge of the trees.

'Now is our chance!' said Jaimie. 'Softly now! Make no sound. We must not aggravate him further.'

They slipped down from the tree and, like two shadows, fled back to the fence. When they were safely on the other side Sheena sank down, fighting to keep back tears of relief. In spite of Jaimie's plaid, which he had retrieved and had placed round her shoulders, she was shivering from head to foot, partly with cold and partly with fright. Jaimie half carried her back to the house and, kicking open the kitchen door with his foot, he laid her down on the old-fashioned settle in front of the fire, while a frightened Mairi and a round-eyed Eppie, both of whom were quite sure he had rescued their mistress from the *each dubh*, helped him to coax the fire into a blaze, and set upon it a huge black kettle.

'Is there enough hot water in the boiler for a bath?'

he demanded. 'Your mistress is nearly frozen.'

'Warm it is, for sure,' answered Mairi, 'but I am thinking it will not be hot enough for a bath. The fire has not been heated up, us not knowing that the young mistress would be for wanting a bath.'

'Oh, very well,' said Jaimie, fully understanding the limitations and vagaries of the hot-water system in ancient Highland dwellings. 'Make some tea for her now, and while she is drinking it we will heat water on the fire for a bath.'

While the great pans of water heated, Jaimie and Sheena drank their tea. Mairi and Eppie tactfully withdrew, leaving herself, as they already called their young mistress, and himself together. Who knew but that the laird might ask herself to marry him? And where would the young mistress find a better match in the whole island than Gordon of Airdrochnish? Was it not rumoured also that he was like to make a great fortune at the film-acting! Yes, Mairi and Eppie were all in favour!

'Well, I shall be leaving you now,' said Jaimie, when they had finished their tea. 'The lassies will be seeing to the hot bath for you, and after that you will be going straight to your bed, I hope, or you will be catching a chill. Your mother, they tell me, is still asleep, so I shall not disturb her. And now, in case I do not see you again before I go to London, I am bidding goodbye to you, my dear. It may be that I shall be home for a short time at Hogmanay, or perhaps not until the spring. You will let me know if you are in any trouble, or in need of help?' He held out his hand and Sheena took it, her eyes downcast. Jaimie smiled to himself, remembering how he had kissed her goodbye, all unbeknown, out in the moonlit field. And Sheena smiled also, because she had recovered consciousness just a few moments before Jaimie realised it, and she knew perfectly well that he had kissed her. She did not say so, however. While she knew something that he did not, she felt she had power over him.

2 IN REGENT'S PARK

Usually Annette leaped up the escalators on the left-hand side, but this evening she joined the staid people who stood at the rail on the right and allowed herself to be carried to the top in leisurely fashion. Oh, her poor feet! She leaned her weight first upon one of them, then upon the other, to rest them. She had had a hard class during the morning, it is true, but it wasn't the class that had tired her. It was the film studios. She'd spent most of her day there, doing absolutely nothing, and it's a well-known fact – there isn't anything quite so tiring as doing nothing.

Life at the moment was certainly rather hectic, thought Annette, as she dived into the subway at Piccadilly Circus. It was one mad rush from the Cosmopolitan School of Ballet to the film studios, and then back again, with no time between to remove make-up, to do one's hair or even to think. And as for meals – she'd had nothing to eat since breakfast, unless you could count a sandwich, half of which she'd had to leave because the film director had decided to shoot a small part of the ballet at that particular moment and had then changed his mind. When Annette got back from the set she found her half-sandwich had disappeared, presumably eaten by some other hungry person, and it didn't seem worthwhile to get another one.

'And now I'll be late for dinner,' she said aloud, as she reached the steps of the convent home where she lived. 'They'll surely have finished by now.' Her forbodings were true – she was just in time to say 'Hello' to the people who were coming out of the refectory.

'I've kept some pudding back for you, dear,' Sister Angelica said kindly. She always had a special smile for the small, lonely girl from far-off Northumberland. Although Annette was fifteen years old she looked a great deal younger, and the nuns of the convent home always treated her as if she were a child. 'It's on a tray in the refectory.'

'Thank you, Sister Angelica,' said Annette faintly. 'I'll go there now.' She limped painfully into the big, empty room and sat down gingerly on a polished wooden bench. If you have never imagined aches and pains in connection with a ballet-dancer, now is the time for your disillusionment. Every bone in Annette's slender body was aching; her feet felt like jellies; even her eyes ached. True, the ballet wasn't responsible for all this, but the fact remained – Annette Dancy neither felt nor looked the least bit like the ballet-dancer she was, nor the glamorous film star she hoped to become. She looked much more like a very tired schoolgirl.

As she stared down at Sister Angelica's tray her hunger left her. A square pile of sturdy sandwiches – a little filling and much bread – was flanked by a slab of cold sponge pudding, covered by a film of pale yellow custard. A fresh wave of weariness engulfed her. She pushed the plate away with a sigh and ran a thin hand through her dark hair. She would go and lie down. But oh, the many flights of stairs she must climb to reach her little room on the fifth floor. The mere thought of them made her bones creak! If only the lift wasn't out of order, but the sad fact was that the lift, which was so old it was nearly falling to pieces, had clanked to a standstill the day before, and didn't look like ever moving again. Workmen had shaken their heads over it and said that it would have to be a new one this time. But a lift costs a lot of money, and funds were definitely short at the convent home, so it looked as if Annette and the other people on the upper floors would have some climbing to do.

But not yet – not yet, thought Annette. I just couldn't tackle five flights of stairs at the moment. I'll go out into the park and get a breath of fresh air. I can sit on a bench, and – yes, she brightened up a little, I can feed the ducks. She packed the sandwiches and the slab of pudding into a paper serviette that lay beside the tray, took a gulp of water and left the refectory.

The echoing corridors of the convent home were

cool, even if the water wasn't. The highly polished parquet floor gleamed like a river, and, reflected in it, was the little statuette of the Virgin and Child that stood at the bottom of the staircase. Someone had placed a vase of white Michaelmas daisies beside it, and they were reflected too. A dreadful flood of homesickness swept over Annette. What would she give, at this moment, to be at home on the high Northumbrian moors, dabbling her tired aching feet in the cool waters of the Mintlaw Burn, and listening to the curlews calling. Most of all she longed to see her darling mother, and Bella, and all her friends.

She shook herself. How stupid to be homesick at a moment like this, when things were going so well for her. Wasn't she dancing the chief role in the ballet *La Sylphide* that was to be in the Scottish film *Pride o' the North*? What more could any budding dancer wish for?

If only there was more dancing in it, thought Annette. And if only it wasn't all so crazy – doing little bits here and there, over and over again, until none of it *means* anything. It was true, you simply couldn't get into the spirit of the ballet, dancing it piecemeal like that. Added to this there were the awful lights and the make-up you had to wear to combat them. How could you feel like a Sylphide, a spirit of the woods, under those conditions, let alone with all the cameramen dashing here, there and everywhere, and shouting at each other until the very moment before the scene was shot? She felt she'd never get used to it. In short, it was clear that Annette didn't think much of the making of films.

She was so deep in her thoughts that she found herself in Regent's Park without knowing how she had got there, though perhaps it was partly due to the fact that her head felt light and her legs weak. But here, at any rate, were the ducks, all quacking cheerfully and looking most expectant. They knew Annette as an old friend for she often came to feed them. She took the packet of sandwiches out of her pocket – Annette never bothered about her appearance off-stage, and it had not occurred to her that a large parcel sticking out of the front of her coat might look at all odd – and spent a happy quarter of an hour watching the antics of the ducks.

One of the park-keepers spent the same length of time watching Annette. He was fascinated not by her beauty, for she had none, but by the variety of expressions that passed over her vivid little face, and most of all by the exquisite grace of her every movement. The air with which she threw her sandwiches to the ducks – well, thought the park-keeper, it was worth something to see! Incidentally, he put Annette down as twelve or thirteen.

'Always wantin' more, them ducks!' he remarked conversationally. 'Inexhaustible, I call 'em. Where they put it all diddles me!'

'Yes, it is rather amazing,' agreed Annette. 'And they're quite shameless, too. Look at that now!' The ducks, seeing that she had come to the end of her provisions, had sailed away, still quacking, tails flicking, to a point farther round the lake where a small boy with a satchel promised more in the feeding line than their former patron.

'Oh, you heartless, fickle things!' cried Annette. 'After all I've given you I do think you might have stayed for a bit and kept me company!'

'Not them!' said the park-keeper. 'There's a lot of 'uman nature in them ducks, if you asks me. The more they gets, the more they bites the 'and that feeds 'em.'

Annette couldn't help laughing. The very idea of ducks biting!

'I do see what you mean,' she said. 'But I can't help liking them, all the same.'

'Well, good day to you, missy,' said the man. He

had revised his opinion of Annette's age. He now put her down as an old-fashioned fourteen. 'And see here,' he added, watching her crumple up her paper bag, 'there's a litter basket just round the corner, so don't you go throwing no bags down on the grass.'

'As if I would!' said Annette indignantly.

As soon as she had disposed of the bag she began to wish she had saved just a little of her dinner for herself after all. Even a couple of doorstep sandwiches would be better than nothing. However, it was too late now – the deed was done and no amount of wishing would bring them back again. She looked longingly at the coffee-stall at the park gates. Should she spend some of her precious allowance on a cup of coffee and a hot dog? She debated the matter, and while she was still hesitating the man inside the stall hailed her.

'Hi, missy! 'Alf a mo!' Then, when Annette had come up to him, he went on, 'Like to do a chap a good turn?'

'That depends,' said Annette cautiously.

'Well, it's like this, see,' said the man. 'The wife is in 'orspital, 'aving an emergency operation. They come and took 'er away in the ambulance early this mornin'. Want to know 'ow she's come through. Anxious time, if you see what I mean, missy.'

'Oh, I *do*!' cried Annette sympathetically. 'Several people in our village have had operations, and, being so isolated, one never knows whether the ambulance will get through the snowdrifts. That's in winter, of course. It's a strange thing how operations always happen in the winter, isn't it? But I don't quite see how I can help you.'

'If you would stay and mind the stall,' said the man, 'while I nip across to the call-box over there –' he nodded at the far side of the road '– I'd be ever so much obliged. I would reely.'

'If I do it, can I have a cup of coffee?' asked Annette, quick to exploit the situation.

'Twenty cups, if you like,' said the man recklessly. He measured up her slender figure, and added, 'And hot dogs too – as many as you like.' After all, he thought, she couldn't eat all that much, and her that slim! Alas, he didn't know the large appetites of ballet-dancers. Before very long he was sadder and wiser!

'All right – I'll do it,' promised Annette. 'But don't be long because it's time I went home. I have a great deal of washing to do – my tights and things.'

In about ten minutes the coffee-stall man was back again, his face wreathed in smiles.

'It's all right!' he shouted at the top of his voice. 'She's come through it fine! They say she'll be 'ome again in a couple of weeks.'

'Oh, I *am* glad,' said Annette. 'You must be relieved. By the way, I've sold four coffees and six hot dogs and a packet of fancy biscuits.'

'You done fine, missy,' said the man admiringly. ''Ave another coffee?'

'No, thank you – I've already had three,' said Annette. 'And I had quite a lot of other things besides. Hot dogs, cheese straws, sandwiches and biscuits. I think that's all – oh, no, I had half a Swiss roll. I do hope it wasn't too much?'

'Not at all, not at all,' said the man, beaming at her. Nothing could upset him now that he knew the missis was okay. All the same, he watched Annette curiously as she walked away, as slender and as light as a fairy. Where did she put it all? – that was what he wanted to know.

3 BALLET-SCHOOL

October drew to a close and Annette's life grew a little less hectic, since the ballet sequences in the film *Pride o' the North* had been shot for the final and last time and the rushes had been approved. The producer was not working on other parts of the film, so Annette and her fellow-sylphs weren't needed at the film studios. As a consequence Annette no longer arrived at her ballet-classes exhausted and unfed, and Monsieur Georges had stopped glowering.

It was strange, thought Annette, to descend from being a film star to a mere junior member of the Georges Reinholt ballet-school; to be shouted at, stormed at, or ignored – according to how the Great Man felt at the moment. She tried hard to think of Taglioni who, when her ballet-master used to throw his stick at her, made a habit of returning it to him meekly with a curtsy! Annette wasn't at all a meek girl, yet she bore all Monsieur Georges's ragings and vituperations without a murmur. All of which goes to show what a great part tradition plays in the art of ballet. Taglioni had put up with Cecchetti's moods and tantrums; so Annette Dancy could put up with *her* temperamental ballet-master's. The fact remains – no shop assistant, secretary or, indeed, any working girl would have endured for a moment the insults hurled at the luckless ballet-students by their fiery, dynamic little ballet-master. Yet they adored him, one and all. For his sake they worked harder and for longer hours than any dock-hand or navvy. To please him they worked in a cold studio on frosty mornings, their limbs covered with gooseflesh, the tips of their noses blue with cold. For Monsieur Georges's sake they went without their meals; sometimes they worked far into the night. On frequent occasions they found themselves going home when other people were starting work!

Yes, it's a strange thing how enthusiasm begets enthusiasm. No one could accuse Monsieur Georges of not believing in what he taught. He lived for his art, and spared himself no more than he spared his dancers. He loved them all, though sometimes, it's true, he was more of a slave-driver than a lover! But then Monsieur Georges was no ordinary lover. His love was not for his pupils themselves, but for the perfection of their dancing, the beauty of their line, the patterns they made with their highly trained and perfect limbs. And they returned his love in the same fashion – Annette especially. She would watch him when he demonstrated the steps and *enchaînements*, and would sigh for the sheer beauty of his finely muscled limbs, his ascetic profile with the highly bridged nose, the deep-set eyes, the haughty carriage of the head. He did not smoke; he did not drink; he ate sparingly. His whole life was dedicated to his beloved art. Yes, it is no exaggeration to say he lived for it.

Usually the ballet-classes were held in the mornings, when members of the company could join in, for the school was essentially run in conjunction with the ballet company, but they went on far into the afternoon with a break for sandwiches and cocoa, tea or coffee, according to taste. Old Arabelle made the latter for the dancers, and brought it to them in squat steaming jugs from her flat on the rooftop. Old Arabelle was as much a slave to the ballet in her way as Monsieur Georges was in his, for she had grown up with the theatre and now acted as wardrobe-mistress to the company, besides being caretaker.

Sometimes Annette took her sandwiches out into one of London's parks or squares and went without her hot drink, but now in this cold weather she was only too glad to drink it in the studio, huddled with the other students round an old iron stove, which was the only form of heating the roof studio possessed. They couldn't afford anything more up to date, and anyway, Monsieur Georges didn't believe in all this central heating. It made the students half asleep, he declared. He preferred to keep his dancers on their toes – literally! Let them get warm by hard work! '*Allons!* to the barres! Begin with pliés – one-and-

two-and-three-and-four-and – Battements *tendus* to the side . . . to the back . . . to the side . . . '

It was amazing how quickly the dancers warmed up. In half an hour they would be rosy-faced, supple of limb. After an hour they would be dripping with perspiration. Out would come the rough towels as they stripped off tights and tunics, and put on their everyday clothes. For them it might well be a summer's day!

But it was in the evening that the building really became alive. While the ballet was performing in the theatre below, the students would be diligently practising and rehearsing once more up in their roof studio.

At the moment the company was rehearsing hard for the opening, on the 26th of December, of *The Little Mermaid*. This was an arrangement for children of the old Hans Andersen fairytale, and it was to be performed, in conjunction with a nearby drama school, by the entire company. There was to be a full-scale ballet in the middle, with choreography by Georges Reinholt Dutoit. The students of the ballet-school were to supplement the company, and were to be given several dances on their own. One of the female roles, that of the Water-witch, would be danced by a man, Charles MacMillan, who had danced James to Annette's La Sylphide on their Scottish tour. Paddy, Annette's Irish friend, had been lucky and had been given one of the Princesses, principally because she happened to be the same size as the other five! The principal role of the Little Mermaid was to be danced by the prima ballerina of the company, a girl named Emma Gautier.

Of course Annette longed and longed to dance the role of the Little Mermaid, but alas, she was relegated to the mere corps de ballet. Monsieur Georges was keeping her to her word. She had said she would cheerfully go back into the corps, and so she should! It would do her good after being fêted and spoilt in the odious film studio. One crumb of consolation did Monsieur Georges fling to his youngest pupil – she could, if she wished, understudy Mlle Gautier as the Little Mermaid. Perhaps he knew that, with his permission, or without it, she would learn completely every lovely flowing movement of the beautiful sea-maiden. It was, thought Annette, the role of her dreams, a role made for her, and Monsieur Georges, watching her, unseen, through the glass door of the studio as she practised, thought so too, but said nothing. It would do Annette Dancy all the good in the world to be kept severely in the background for a while. She had been in the limelight a great deal too much of late – she would be getting, as Monsieur Georges called it, swollen of the head. He disapproved of this film business. Annette must realise that she was not a film star, nor a prima ballerina – no, not even yet a ballerina, but merely just a little dancer!

4 JAIMIE IN LONDON

Surprisingly enough Jaimie had never been to London. He had done his training as a veterinary surgeon at Edinburgh University and, like most Scotsmen, his view was that, whatever the capital of England had to offer, the capital of Scotland had much more!

He had been in London now for a week and, although working in the same studios, and on the same film, as Annette, he had never once caught sight of her. This was not surprising, of course, since she had finished her work on the film sequences. It had not occurred to Jaimie to ask Mamie Slaughter for Annette's address. He had imagined that he would meet her at the film studios, or at any rate that he had only to ask for her. But the studios were unexpectedly vast and full of people, all very busy, and all shouting at the top of their voices, or so it seemed to Jaimie. The first person he asked – one of the cameramen – looked blank. Annette Dancy? He seemed to think he'd heard the name somewhere . . . Oh, yes, of course! The kid in the ballet film. Nice kid. Lovely dancer, too, though he did prefer tap to ballet himself. Her address? Sorry – hadn't a clue. What about Charlie? Charlie ought to know . . . 'Hi, Charlie! D'yer know where the kiddie –' like everyone else they thought Annette was about fourteen '– who dances La What's-its-name in *Pride o' the North* hangs out?'

Charlie shook his head.

'Sorry, old chap. Haven't an earthly. Try Jimmy. Trust Jimmy to know where all the pretty girls live!'

But Annette wasn't old enough, or didn't look old enough, to attract the flirtatious Jimmy. Or perhaps she wasn't pretty enough. Anyway, although he knew her by sight, he had no idea of her address.

After Jaimie had tried about eight or nine people and met with no success, he gave it up as a bad job and decided to write home to Mamie for Annette's address. And then, as so often happens, when he had quite stopped looking for her, and wasn't even thinking about her, he saw her. Something had gone wrong in one of the ballet sequences they had already shot, so Annette had received a summons to be at the studios for a retake. She was sitting on a packing-case, watching with interest a group of people dressed in what Jaimie called 'fancy dress'. They were obviously having a breather between shots. Two of them, at least, were famous film stars – so famous that anyone but Jaimie Gordon, of the remote Island of Skye, would have recognised them instantly and would have been duly awe-stricken. The lady, dark and vivacious, with a small heart-shaped face and green eyes, wore a long velvet cloak edged with ermine; her companion – also dark, with black curls and slumberous eyes, and an attractive sulky expression – was encased from head to foot in a glittering suit of armour. He was minus a helmet, the omission being due, no doubt, to the extreme heat of the studios, and to the fact that he was smoking. The lady was enjoying a cigarette too, and very strange it looked, thought Annette, to see the smoke wreathing round her wimple! So fascinated was she by the sight that, when a soft voice spoke her name in her ear, she almost jumped out of her skin.

'*Jaimie*! You nearly frightened me to death! Where

have you been all this time? I've looked for you everywhere, but I expect they haven't been doing the bit of the film you're in. It's all quite mad –' she shrugged her shoulders expressively '– like Alice in Wonderland, and it's my opinion they don't know themselves what they're doing. Take me, for instance. I'd finished my sequences, and then this morning I got an urgent phone call to come here for a retake; some of the rushes weren't satisfactory, I suppose. Well, here I am, and here I've been all day, and we haven't done a thing so far, and now it's time to go home. I've missed a most important rehearsal too – at my dancing-school, I mean – and Monsieur Georges will be growling like a tiger!'

'I've been looking for you too,' said Jaimie. They compared notes and laughed together as they left the vast buildings and stood waiting for a bus. Several passed them without stopping, but at last one drew up and, although it looked full, they managed to squeeze on board. The bus lurched away, and Jaimie and Annette were flung into each other's arms. Wildly they clutched the rails, and Jaimie, looking down at Annette's pale, weary face, felt his blood boil. What Highlander would occupy a seat while a small, white-faced, weary lassie hung on a pole? If he had been at home in Skye he could have done something about it, but here . . . Yes, he *could* do something! At the next stop he astonished Annette by bending down and whispering in her ear, 'It is here that we will get down.'

'Oh, but it's not the right stop,' expostulated Annette. 'This is only Trafalgar Square.'

'We will get down here,' repeated Jaimie firmly. He proceeded to astonish Annette still further by announcing, 'We will take a taxi to where I am staying, and then we will have a meal together – that is, if you can spare the time,' he added, remembering that Annette was a working girl. 'I am staying at the YMCA,' he told her.

Annette wasn't so surprised at this announcement as some people might have been. She knew that Jaimie would never spend his money before he got it. At the present moment he had very little in the bank, although it's true that at no very distant date he would receive what amounted to a small fortune for his work on the film he was making. But he hadn't got it yet. Moreover, he didn't see anything wrong with the YMCA hostel. The food was good; he had a bed to sleep in, the fact that it was hard didn't worry Jaimie – he had never slept in a soft one anyway: he had a cubicle all to himself. What more could any young man want? As for Annette, she merely exclaimed, 'But, Jaimie, if you mean the YM in Crawford Street, why the bus goes right past it. We needn't have got off.'

'I am thinking it is time you sat down,' said Jaimie in his soft, unhurried Highland voice. Then the taxi he had hailed stopped and they got in. It must be explained here that Jaimie thoroughly disapproved of the taxi habit. Why take a taxi and pay through the nose for it, argued the young man, when you could walk upon your own feet, and see more of your surroundings besides? But he recognised the need for it in Annette's case. He was careful in money matters, but who dare call him mean when, at the end of the ride, he withdrew from his slender notecase a five-pound note and paid the driver without a murmur what he considered an outrageous sum for a few minutes' ride? No one, I think!

They had a wonderful supper of Irish stew, with lots of onions and potatoes. Sitting at a small table in the big, cheerful, noisy dining-room of the YMCA they talked together of old times and old acquaintances – Annette, it may be said, doing most of the talking. Although there were no hovering waiters, and you had to shout to make yourself heard, Annette was thrilled with everything. Perhaps being with Jaimie, who knew all her friends, made a difference. She heard from him how Pop Slaughter had become an expert fisherman; how Mamie had been persuaded to discard her high-heeled shoes and put on strong boots, and had become quite an ardent hiker. She heard that in May the film personnel, not including the dancers for the ballet sequences, of course, would go on location in Skye, ready for the shooting of the climbing parts of the film.

'We are taking over the Youth Hostel at Glen Brittle,' said Jaimie, 'and from there we shall do several spectacular climbs – a rescue on the Inaccessible Pinnacle on Sgurr Dearg and a climb on A'Cioch, which is a great buttress of rock that sticks out from the main precipices of Sgumain. In order to shoot these scenes we shall have to make use of many local climbers besides myself and Angus. Oh, yes – Angus is to be given special leave from school to do this.'

'Oh, dear! You're making me want to be there!' cried Annette. 'But of course I couldn't afford it, even if I weren't far too busy.'

After they had finished their meal they walked back to Annette's convent home. The girl's face was no longer white and drawn, and her step had regained its buoyancy. She possessed that quality, essential to a ballet-dancer, the power to recover quickly from her weariness.

5 MADAME TUSSAUD'S

In theory, Saturday was a day off for the students of the Cosmopolitan School of Ballet, but, in actual fact, there was usually a rehearsal or a class of some sort that hadn't been able to be squeezed in during the week. On the Saturday before Christmas, however, Annette met her brother, Max, on the steps of her convent home with a jubilant, 'Nothing to do all day, Maxie, my sweet! I can take as long as ever I want over my lunch, and know I'm not going to be late for anything. What luxury! Oh, Max – what shall we do? We must make the most of it. Have you got the whole day too?'

'Nearly,' answered Max, as they strode away in the direction of Oxford Circus. 'I'm on tonight but only in the second half of the programme, so I needn't be at the theatre until about seven.'

'As a matter of fact,' confessed Annette, 'I've got a Greek class at half past six – I was trying hard to forget about it. I don't think Greek dancing is my line, but Monsieur Georges insists that it helps the classical ballet. One becomes a little tight and strained with nothing but classical, so he says.' Annette always talked in a very old-fashioned and grown-up manner when she was discussing ballet technique. 'But one can hardly call half past six *today*,' she added. 'I still feel I've got *today* free. I've put my Greek tunic on under my coat,' she went on, 'and Monsieur Georges doesn't mind bare legs – I mean for the class – so I'm all ready. I needn't go back a minute before twenty-five past six . . . Oh, dear, I'm forgetting about my washing.'

'Your washing?' repeated Max, puzzled.

'Yes, I'm afraid I have some to do. It's just a pair of tights for Monday, and if I could wash them through in the bathroom and hang them up in my room it would be easy; but you see I have to go right down to the laundry – six flights of stairs and six back –'

'Why?' interrupted her brother. 'Seems batty to me – just for one pair of tights.'

'Yes, doesn't it?' agreed Annette. 'Some people are odd – they don't like to see even a pair of tights hung up to dry, especially on Sunday, and it's awkward because Saturday is my most free day.'

'But I didn't know anyone *could* see them,' said Max. 'I mean, I didn't know there were any houses opposite the home. I thought they were all offices.'

'So they are – almost all,' said Annette, as they dived into the Underground. 'But one person does live there, and it's her that complains.'

'Well, why didn't you explain to her?' said Max.

'I couldn't,' said Annette, 'because she complained to the Mother Superior, who passed it on to Sister Angelica who told me about it, so you see it was at least third hand. But you see how it is? I must do my washing in the laundry in the future, even if it does take longer.'

'Look, Annette,' said Max, as they reached the ticket machines, 'you've rushed me down here, and we don't even know where we're going.'

'Yes, we do,' contradicted Annette. 'We're going to Madame Tussaud's. I took dear Jaimie there last week, but I don't think he was very impressed. Of course he didn't actually say so – he's much too polite – but I could tell by the way he thanked me afterwards that he didn't really think much of it. He "prefaired" real history to wax, and of course you can understand it when you know where he lives. Highland chieftains are always like that, aren't they?'

'I haven't a clue,' said Max. 'Never met any – except Jaimie . . .'

'Well, I simply couldn't get darling Jaimie to browse in the Chamber of Horrors,' went on Annette. 'I expect he's had too many horrors in Skye – I mean in the past, of course – so he doesn't need any wax ones to make him shiver. But it's a fact – it takes a long time to catch the atmosphere down there. Oh, Max, let's go and see darling Henry the Eighth and all his wives. I love Henry, don't you? I think he's a duck!'

'You wouldn't think so if you were one of his

womenfolk,' declared Max. 'It would be case of "Off with her head!" in no time at all with you! Henry wouldn't have stood five minutes of *you*, Annette Dancy, I can tell you. You're too forthright.'

'What do you mean?' demanded Annette haughtily, as they boarded a west-bound train.

'You say what you think without thinking,' explained Max. 'It never pays – I should say paid, shouldn't I? Well, here we are. Only one station. Can't think why you dragged me down here!'

'Neither can I, come to that,' admitted Annette. 'I must have been thinking about something else.'

'That's highly likely,' observed her brother.

Five minutes later they arrived outside the building that housed Madame Tussaud's exhibition.

'I want two tickets, please,' said Max to the man in the ticket-office. 'One for me and one for my little sister.' He gave Annette a wink as the man handed out a half-ticket 'for the kiddie'.

'Angus would be horrified,' declared Annette. 'Me getting in under false pretences.'

'Okay. You go back and tell him you're over age,' said Max. 'I've done my best for you. Anyway neither of us told any lies – he just assumed you were a kid, so it's his fault.'

'If I were richer I should go back and tell him,' said Annette, 'me being a clergyman's daughter, but just now I'm too hard up. I'm pretty sure I'm much harder up than Madame Tussaud, whoever she is.'

'She's dead, idiot,' said Max.

'In that case it can't really matter to her if I get in for half-price,' said Annette happily, and she skipped along in front of her brother, her eyes shining with anticipation of the delights in store.

'Yes,' said Max, going back to the discussion of behaviour in days of old, 'you had to be subtle in those days if you wanted to survive . . . Come on, this way, if you want to see King Henry and his harem! There you are! What's the matter?' Annette was staring at Ann Boleyn's pretty face with a shocked expression. It was obvious she was back in Tudor times, and her ever-vivid imagination at work.

'Oh, the poor darling!' she exclaimed. 'Oh, Maxie – fancy anyone cutting off *her* head. I can't bear to think of it! I don't think I like Henry after all! Let's go, Max. I've had enough of olden times . . . I wonder if they've got Anna Pavlova – in wax, I mean? Or Margot Fonteyn? Let's ask that policeman.' She ran across to a burly officer, Max close behind her.

'Please, could you tell us . . .' Then they both began to laugh. The 'policeman' was a waxwork!

'Oh, dear!' Annette said with a sigh. 'Come on – let's be off to the Chamber of Horrors and have a good shiver before it's time for lunch.'

They spent a long time in the Chamber of Horrors. As Annette said – it was gloriously creepy.

'Almost too creepy,' she added, stopping to gaze at a notorious murderer. 'Oh, Max, wouldn't it be a joke if he wasn't a waxwork at all – if he was a criminal fleeing from justice, and had come in here to evade the law, and was just pretending to be a waxwork? He looks awfully real, don't you think? You can see his eyes glittering and following you round. I dare you to touch him, Max.'

'What, me?' said Max with a shudder. 'Against the rules to poke waxworks!'

'Pooh!' said Annette. 'You're scared.'

'All right – do it yourself, then.'

'No thank you,' said Annette. 'Come on, Max. Let's go up again where it isn't quite so spooky. I feel this place is full of people –'

'Well, so it is – wax people.'

'Yes, but not wax. I feel they're all alive and watching us. Let's go quickly!'

They fled from the shadowy Chamber of Horrors to the more cheerful halls above, and stood for a while looking at Danny Kaye and Bob Hope. Two women came through the doorway, talking and laughing. Upon a sudden mischievous impulse, Annette slipped off her coat and shoes and dived under the rail. Standing on the daïs, in her dancing tunic, she froze into a Greek attitude. Max, ever ready to aid and abet his sister, especially if she happened to be doing something wicked, entered into the spirit of the thing and walked gravely round her, studying her from every angle.

'Goodness!' exclaimed one of the women with a giggle. 'I thought for a moment she was real! It just goes to show.'

'Yes, it does, doesn't it?' said Max. 'It's amazing how alive these waxworks can look. I thought she was real myself until a moment ago, but when I looked more closely I saw, of course, that she was a replica of Margot Fonteyn all right. Splendid likeness too, don't you think? Beautiful girl, eh?'

The two women walked slowly round Annette and considered the matter of her beauty.

'No, I can't say I think she's pretty, exactly,' said the elder of the two. 'But I agree there's something about her – if you see what I mean. Funny, though, I never imagined Margot Fonteyn would look like that off-stage.'

Suddenly the younger woman gave a squeal.

'I could swear she moved! She blinked an eyelid – I swear she did!'

'Nonsense, Dorothea! How could she?' said her

companion severely. 'You let your imagination run away with you. Blink an eyelid, indeed!'

But just at this moment Annette did more than blink an eyelid. She completely overbalanced and fell in a heap upon the floor at the feet of the petrified women. Their hysterical screams brought a caretaker running.

'I'm sorry! I'm *so* sorry!' said Annette through gales of laughter. 'I didn't mean to frighten you – honestly I didn't.'

Presently the women began to laugh as well, together with a little crowd of sightseers who had come running out of the other halls when they heard the uproar.

'But don't you do it again, missy,' said the caretaker, trying to sound severe. 'It's all very well for waxworks to stand around pretending to be real, but to 'ave real people pretending to be waxworks – well, it might be dangerous, see? People with weak 'earts, and what not. Understand, missy? Don't you go doin' it again.'

'All right, I won't,' promised Annette. 'Maxie won't let me, will you, Max?'

'*Non pas!*' said Max, putting on his most severe expression. '*Je vous en dit.*'

The caretaker stared at Max and Annette, as they walked out of the gallery, then winked at the two women.

'French – the young man, anyway! That explains it!'

6 ANNETTE GOES HOME

November had slipped away and it was now well into December. Just over a week to Christmas! The ballet students began to discuss their plans.

'We've all of Christmas Eve and all of Christmas Day,' said French Marie. 'For me, I am wondering if I could fly to Paris to make the visit to my peoples.'

'But of course you could,' cried Annette. 'Why, Paris is much nearer than where I'm going. I'm going all the way back to my home up in Northumberland. Oh, I know I'll only have two days there – even if I manage to catch the midnight train after the dress-rehearsal – but it'll be worth it.'

'And your so good-looking brother – goes he with you?' asked Marie. Max had been to watch several of the classes and rehearsals and they had seen him dance his famous farucca, so they all knew him.

'Oh, no,' said Annette with a sigh. 'You see Max opens – I mean his company opens – on Christmas Night at Torquay, and from Newcastle to Torquay is twice as far as from Newcastle to London, so it's quite impossible. That's the worst of a dancing career – you spend Christmas in such odd places! But oh, it would have been lovely if we could have spent Christmas all together.' She sighed again.

'Och, mavourneen – you must not be sad!' exclaimed Paddy. 'Sure, and it's worse for me, it is, for I can't get to my home in Killarney at all, at all, and it's in London I shall be spending my Christmas.'

'Oh, Paddy, I'm so sorry!' Annette was all contrition. 'Here am I doing nothing but think about myself, and you with nowhere to lay your poor head. Why not come home with me, Paddy? You can have my bedroom, and I'll sleep on the settee in the Round Lounge. We haven't any spare bedrooms, you see, now that the peel-tower has been divided.'

'Och, no, thank you a thousand times all the same,' said Paddy. 'I have me friends in London, and it's they who have invited me to spend Christmas with them, so it's all right I'll be.'

And now you can imagine the letters that flew from London to Northumberland, and from Northumberland to London. The first was from Annette to her mother:

Darling Mummy,

Most exciting news! I think *I'm going to be able to come home for Christmas. Our Christmas show,* THE LITTLE MERMAID, *opens on the 26th of December – that's the day after Christmas Day – and rehearsals finish on the 23rd, so we'll have the whole of Christmas*

Eve and the whole of Christmas Day free. I'll catch the midnight train from King's Cross after the dress-rehearsal, and if someone could possibly meet me I could be home in time for breakfast. Think of it! If not, I can get a bus to Winshiel and walk from there. It's only three or four miles, so I could do it easily. Oh, Mummy, I'm so excited I can hardly wait – though Christmas is less than a fortnight away! It seems years and years since I saw you all, and the darling Peel.

I wonder if Angus will be home for Christmas, or if he'll be in Skye, or somewhere? Please write quickly and tell me all the news. On second thoughts you needn't bother, because I'll be home and I'll hear it for myself. Oh, that sounds as if I didn't want you to write, but you know I don't mean that, don't you, darling? I just live to get your letters!

Love as ever from
Annette.

In a very few days' time Annette received an answer from her mother.

Dancing Peel,
10th Dec. (Old Sally Muirhead's birthday)

My dearest,

We are all thrilled to hear you will be coming home for Christmas – even though it is for so short a time.

There isn't much news here, except of course that the alterations to the peel are nearly finished, and will be quite done by Christmas – even the tower. The vicar has got nicely settled into his new quarters in the north wing, and that leaves plenty of rooms for us. Your little bedroom is just the same, and we still have the Round Lounge. The main staircase is in the vicar's part, and that leaves the old stone one for us. I know you'll be glad, because you can still climb up on to the roof that way.

I've been asked by everyone in the village to ask you if you would dance at the usual Christmas Eve 'hop' in the Parish Hall? Everyone would be so thrilled if you would.

Angus's school breaks up on the 20th, and he is spending Christmas with his father at the peel, so we shall be a merry party! I thought, perhaps, that Angus's cousin, Sheena, would be here too (you know she lost her mother, poor girl, a short time ago), but I had a letter from Mrs Slaughter, whom you stayed with in Skye last summer, and she says that Sheena will probably be staying with them at the castle over Christmas. Deborah Slaughter will be home from her Swiss school for the holidays, so they will be company for each other.

Write quickly, my darling, to say whether you will dance for the village cause they want to put it on the posters. It will be a great attraction!

Lots of love as ever,

Mummy.

*　　*　　*

Annette had got it all worked out. After the dress-rehearsal on the Tuesday she would catch the mid-night train from King's Cross to Newcastle. Of course, the rehearsal would go on and on, they always do, but she'd manage it somehow.

As usual, when everything looks like plain sailing there proved to be stormy water ahead. Annette's mother refused point-blank to allow her fifteen-year-old daughter to travel alone through the night unless she was safely tucked up in a sleeping-car along with several other people of her own sex. But where was the extra money to come from? That was the knotty question. It had been hard enough to raise the ordinary fare, thought Annette ruefully as she read her mother's second letter, and now all this extra had to be found for the sleeper. You might think that Annette, along with all the other students of the Cosmopolitan School of Ballet, would have made plenty of extra money when on their northern tour. But the plain fact was that the tour, as so often happens, hadn't even paid for itself, and could not have survived had it not been for a grant from the Arts Council. Annette had received a small sum weekly, but that had all gone on digs, ballet-shoes, tights and extra meals. To be sure, she would be well paid for the film she was making. In fact, after the commission paid to the ballet-school had been deducted quite a large sum had already been given into the safe keeping of her trustees, and had been invested for her until she reached the age of eighteen. At the moment, however, Annette Dancy was broke, and no one, not even her mother, could touch that money, unless it was for her education or for some real emergency. A Christmas holiday in Northumberland didn't come under either category – or so it seemed at first. Fortunately Monsieur Georges knew that Annette would go home, no matter what he or anyone else said – even if she had to travel in the guard's van or curl herself up in the luggage-rack without a ticket, or, more likely if she sat up all night – so he moved heaven and earth to help her. Letters flew from the dusty solicitor's office in London to Annette's mother in her remote country peel-tower, and back again to London. Forms were signed, and finally a cheque was issued, signed by the trustees, for an amount which paid not only for the sleeper but the railway fare as well.

'Oh, *good*!' said Annette, with a sigh of relief when she saw it. 'Now I can give back to Mummy the railway fare she sent me.' She never thought of spending the surplus on a new coat for herself as some girls would have done, but then new clothes meant nothing to Annette, so this wasn't as much to her credit as it seems at first glance.

As always, the dress-rehearsal looked as if it was never going to end. Ten o'clock came and went, the theatre came out, and still, up among the rooftops, the tireless students worked at the new ballet. They had already had one rehearsal in the actual theatre, so this was a dress-rehearsal, in actual fact. But of course

Monsieur Georges took the opportunity of getting in a lot more practice, and altering several scenes at the last minute, until the little company was in despair. Why, oh, why did he have to alter the Little Mermaid's dance so that she made that peculiar movement with her hands after each bar of music instead of on the beat? How difficult!

But how much more lovely, and unusual, thought Annette, the understudy, as she waited in the wings – an arrangement of screens. So entranced was she by the movement that she practised it on the spot, with Monsieur Georges's chair for a partner, and nearly forgot to come in for her own 'Dance of the Cockle-shells'. She almost forgot about the time too, and when at length she glanced at her wristwatch, Monsieur Georges having declared the rehearsal to be at an end, she nearly collapsed. It was a quarter to eleven!

Fortunately she had packed her little case that morning and brought it along with her to the ballet-school, so that all she had to do was to grab her coat, not bothering to take off tights or make-up, and set off, helter-skelter, down the six flights of stone stairs in a mad dash for the Underground. Charles MacMillan, who danced the Prince in the ballet, careered along behind her, carrying her case.

'Darling Charles,' panted Annette, 'I do wish you wouldn't do it. You'll miss your own bus, and I can manage easily myself.'

Charles took not the slightest notice, knowing

Annette and her headlong ways. She'd probably go to the wrong station or catch the wrong train!

'Have you got your ticket?' he demanded, as they leaped up the escalator. Annette felt in her pocket – the pocket without the hole in it – and triumphantly displayed the precious little bit of cardboard.

'Well, mind you don't lose it,' cautioned Charles as they emerged from the Underground and raced across to the main station. 'And there's your sleeper ticket to pick up. Got your money?'

Annette produced her purse.

'Well, you *have* been business-like,' admitted Charles. 'I wouldn't have believed it!'

Suddenly Annette stood still on the platform, causing a porter riding on a trolley to swerve violently and then hurl abuse at her. Her face was tragic.

'Charles! The most awful thing has happened – I've forgotten my toothbrush, my hairbrush and all my

washing things! I meant to put them in after I'd finished washing, but I forgot.'

'Oh, well, that won't matter,' said Charles, with a sigh of relief. Judging by Annette's face, it might have been something a lot worse! 'Lots of people don't bother to clean their teeth and wash in a sleeping-car.'

'Yes, I can always buy some toothpaste at the village shop,' said Annette, her face clearing. 'And anyway, I expect Mummy has some, and a hairbrush too . . . Well, here we are. I'm number seven, so I'll be quite all right. Goodbye, dear Charles, and thank you for coming . . . Your bus!'

'Oh, I'll catch it, never fear!' Charles said, and felt it was worth it, even if he didn't. Something in Annette's youth and helplessness had awakened an unexpected streak of chivalry in Charles. As a matter of fact, although Annette had a habit of forgetting tickets and money, and getting herself into awkward predicaments generally, she wasn't nearly as helpless as Charles and other people imagined. She usually managed to come out on top.

Clutching her case, she squeezed down the corridor and found her compartment. In it were two large women, busy undressing. Suddenly, and without the slightest warning, the train began to move out of the station, and Annette was thrown violently against the nearest occupant.

'Oh, I'm s-sorry!' she gasped, lurching backwards into the corridor again.

'I think, if you don't mind, little girl, you had better

stay out there until we're ready for bed,' said the woman. 'There really isn't room for you in here just now. I'll let you know when you can come in.' She slid the door shut firmly, and Annette was left outside, still clutching her case.

Presently the sleeping-car attendant came along the corridor, tapped at the door of the sleeper, and shouted in one breath, 'Tickets-please-tea-in-the-morning-ladies-seven-sharp-must-be-off-the-train-by-half-past. Same for you, missie?'

'What time does the train get into Newcastle?' asked Annette.

'About six o'clock, missie,' answered the man. 'Thanks, madam!' The sleeper door had opened a crack and two tickets were passed out to him.

'I want my tea at a quarter to six then,' said Annette. 'And here is my ticket.'

'A quarter to six?' repeated the attendant and, by the tone of his voice, Annette knew from past experience that he was about to start asking questions, so she put on her most grown-up air.

'Yes, and please do not be late,' she said. 'My friends will be there and I do not wish to keep them waiting.'

'Okay, miss,' he promised. 'A quarter to, it is. Goodnight, miss.'

'Goodnight,' said Annette regally. 'I hope you sleep well.'

The sleeping-car attendant was so taken aback that he forgot to give her his customary wink.

It was some little time before the compartment door slid open again, and when it did a head came out, bristling with curlers, half hidden under a pale-blue net sleeping-cap.

'You can come in now.'

Annette went in, not without difficulty, owing to the fact that the compartment was almost completely filled up by two large suitcases and the stepladder which gave access to the upper berths. On a peg just inside the door hung a shaggy rusty-brown fur coat, which swung to and fro drunkenly. Like a bear on the prowl, thought Annette. Oh, well, I certainly can't undress down here. She hauled herself and her case aloft with the help of the stepladder, and sat down on the edge of the berth, her legs dangling.

No one who hasn't tried would believe how difficult it is to undress in an upper sleeping-berth – even for anyone as small as Annette. Most of her garments came off over her head, so they were easy enough; but her tights were the difficulty. She thought of leaving them on, but the compartment was so hot and stuffy that she decided against it. Finally she managed to wriggle them off somehow and get into her pyjamas. Fortunately the bunk opposite was unoccupied, so she was able to throw all her clothes on to it.

The two large women were already snoring, so she turned off the light and curled herself up in the one rug provided, which wasn't quite wide enough to tuck in at both sides, though it enfolded her feet neatly at the bottom. But alas, tired though she was, she couldn't go to sleep. For one thing, she was much too excited. She tossed and turned on the hard bunk, and finally lay on her back, gazing wide-awake at the dim blue light in the ceiling and listening to the bumping of the fur coat swinging on its hanger, just beside her left ear. Sometimes the train plunged into a tunnel with a dull roar and an unearthly shriek, and always there was the whirring of the wheels and the grinding and squeaking of the couplings as it fled northwards.

Annette must have slept at last, however, for she suddenly woke up feeling deadly cold. A thrill ran through her. They had left the warm southern counties, she thought, and were already in the cold grey north that spelled 'home' to her! The actual fact was that one of the women below had discovered a pipe belching forth hot air and steam right under her berth, had promptly stretched out a ponderous arm and switched the heating to OFF. Whereupon the carriage grew cold – as cold as an unheated railway carriage can be in the middle of a winter's night. There seems to be no happy medium – you either boil or you freeze! Added to this, the rug had slipped its moorings and exposed most of Annette's back to a blast of cold air coming from some unknown place. She discovered later it was the air ventilator in the roof. One thing was certain – she must have more clothes. But how to get them without waking the two sleepers below? – that was the question. She lay shivering while she thought about it, then, cautiously

leaning up on one elbow and stretching out one slender and finely muscled leg across the intervening space between the two top berths, she managed to hook up her tights and another garment which, by great good luck, turned out to be her jumper. Having pulled these on top of her pyjamas, she snuggled down into her rug again and lay waiting until the warmth seeped back into her veins. And then, just as she grew really warm and was sleeping soundly, she was awakened rudely by the light snapping on and a voice below her proclaiming:

'Here y'are, missy – tea! Quarter to six. We're just coming into Newcastle.'

Annette sprang up, wide awake in a flash.

'Newcastle! Oh . . . !'

She took the tea up on the berth; then pulled aside the blind a crack and looked out. It was still dark, but there was a radiance over the sky in the east that showed the dawn wasn't far off. A covering of snow made enough light for her to see the rows of little houses sliding past, each with drawn blinds, like eyelids over sleeping eyes. She turned back to her tea and drank it quickly, while the train slowly rocked to a standstill, jerked backwards for a short way, as if it had suddenly changed its mind, then stopped for good. She was here! She was home again! Feverishly crunching the biscuits that lay in the saucer, for she was hungry, having had no supper the night before, she began to dress.

It was even more difficult dressing in the upper berth than it had been undressing. In the end she had to climb down the ladder to put on her skirt. She needn't have worried – the women remained two humps under their rugs, neither of them stirring, while she collected her belongings, pushed them into her case, and softly left the compartment.

After splashing cold water on her face and drying it on a couple of paper towels, she stepped down on to the platform. She was at the far end, and above her she could see the sky – a cold pale blue, with the stars still winking frostily in it. The station was almost deserted, except for a couple of porters wheeling trolleys and a ticket-collector, who came out of his little box when she appeared and took her ticket, blinking sleepily and swinging his arms to keep warm.

She wasn't being met until eight o'clock, so she had nearly two whole hours before her. She deposited her case at the left-luggage office and set off up Grainger Street. The city was still asleep and not a soul was stirring except a policeman who was standing outside a telephone box. He gave Annette a suspicious glance but said nothing. It was obvious from her purposeful bearing that, young as she was, she knew where she was going. And so she did! This was her one chance of revisiting her beloved city – on her return journey she'd be rushing madly to catch her train. Funny to think that, although it was only six o'clock in the morning, this was Christmas Eve!

And now Annette had reached the top of Grainger Street and was standing looking up at the monument of Earl Grey. She and Angus had once climbed to the top, she remembered as she crossed the square. On and on she walked, up Northumberland Street and into St Mary's Place, where the trees round the church door were hung with coloured electric lights which swung and twinkled in the light breeze. Presently she left the city behind and was in the suburbs, and now here was the Eleanor Brandon School of Dancing, with a cushion of snow over the well-known brass plate at the side of the door. The windows of the big studio on the first floor were frosted over, which meant there had been a hard class last night, thought Annette, and the room had grown hot and steamy. Above the studio were the dormer windows of the little flat where her beloved Nellie

Brandon would at this very moment be sleeping. Annette blew her a kiss and then turned to retrace her steps. It was – she consulted her wristwatch – good gracious, it was a quarter past seven! In exactly three-quarters of an hour they'd be at the station to meet her. She must hurry or she'd be late!

In the last half-hour the sleeping city had awakened. The early buses were careering down the streets, where now many more black footprints crossed Annette's own. Her footsteps quickened as she came within sight of the station . . . A quarter to eight – and just driving under the portico was an old car with a familiar look about it . . . Yes, it was the vicar's, Mr MacCrimmon's car! She ran across the square and disappeared into the station in search of her friends.

'Mummy! Angus! Mr MacCrimmon! Oh, Mummy, Mummy, it's me!' she panted running alongside. 'Oh, how lovely it is just to see you all again! How wonderful to be here!' She tumbled into the back of the car, and only remembered when they had emerged from under the portico that her case was still lying in the left-luggage office. So Angus got out and retrieved it, and after that all was plain sailing.

Westgate Hill lay before them, and up they climbed, changing gear several times, for the gallant little Ford carried four grown-ups and Annette's case, though really, thought Angus as he looked at Annette, she looked as if a puff of wind would blow her away! Yes, she grew more beautiful each time he saw her . . .

7 CHRISTMAS EVE

What, you might well ask, has a remote Northumbrian village, hidden in a fold of the Border moorland, to offer in the way of Christmas festivities? To answer that question you must come with me to Mintlaw. It is evening, and Christmas Eve. A pale moon and a scatter of frosty stars look down upon the little village. The warmth inside the cottages has melted the snow upon the roofs, and only that of the church remains untouched and white, like a Christmas card.

On the north side of the village, glinting in the moonlight, and running sluggishly through the dead rushes and heather as if it knows it will be frozen and silent on the morrow, flows the Mintlaw burn. Dominating the village with its rugged strength stands the ancient peel-tower – Dancing Peel – its roof silhouetted starkly against the pale wintry sky. Eight hundred Christmas Eves has the old Border fortress seen come and go – many of them a great deal less peaceful than this one!

Over on the other side of the village green stands the church with its graceful steeple, pointing the way to heaven. Not far from it is a long, low building, the door of which opens to let out a flood of warmth and light. This is the village hall, and old Martha Keenleside is getting it 'hotted up' for the village hop which is going to take place later in the evening and which will go on till close upon midnight, when the dancers will troop across to the church for the Christmas Mass. Their numbers will be swelled by the carol-singers, who will have been out with their storm-lanterns, singing their songs of goodwill at all the out-bye farms and shepherds' cottages and tiny hamlets out on the lonely hills.

The carol-singers' voices sound thin and reedy in the cold clear air, and the children, just off to bed, their stockings hung up at the bottoms of their beds or at the corners of the mantelpieces, look out from behind the curtains and join in the singing.

And now let us go into the old peel-tower and climb the twisting stone staircase to the little bedroom where Annette Dancy is arraying herself in tights and snowy tutu, ready for her appearance at the village hop.

As we know, the peel-tower has been divided, but Annette's little bedroom remains unchanged. On the far side of the narrow little room is a window, built into the thickness of the wall and reached by two stone steps, which looks out towards the Border. There is another one, rather larger and facing south, through which you may see Mintlaw village green, with the church, and the little cottages clustered round it like chickens round a hen! The church has a warlike look about it, despite its graceful steeple which, by the way, is a later addition. It is roofed by great stone slabs and supported by stone buttresses, nearly as broad as they are long. Truly a difficult building to raze to the ground, a fate only too common to churches a few hundred years ago on the Border! The church is flanked by a graveyard full of ancient moss-grown headstones.

Annette has finished dressing by now, and stands before her looking-glass – a slender dark-eyed girl, with a rather sad little face, though why she should look sad, goodness knows, for her life up to now has been happy enough.

'Mummy! Have you seen my old tweed coat?' she calls from the top of the twisting stone stairway. Although, as we know, she is fifteen years old, she is still a child in many ways. So thinks Angus MacCrimmon, as he stands at the bottom of the stairs looking up at her. In her short frilly tutu she looks about twelve!

The old tweed coat having been found, Annette goes downstairs to be escorted across to the village hall by her mother, the vicar and the vicar's son – not to mention Bella, who 'does' for them at the peel.

'I do hope you aren't too tired, my dear,' says the vicar, looking anxiously at Annette, so slim, so ethereal.

'Oh, no! I'm not tired at all now,' answers Annette. 'It's so lovely to be home again.'

Having met her at the station, they had arrived at Mintlaw in time for a late breakfast. Annette's first sight of her beloved peel-tower home had been through a flurry of snowflakes, which had died away during the afternoon. Oh, how she had hung out of the car window to catch a first glimpse of the old familiar landmarks! Here was the little stone bridge over the burn, and Martha Keenleside's ducks, nothing daunted by the icy water, waddling off towards the farm.

As they drove slowly into the village, the cottage doors flew open and out came all Annette's friends. They all crowded round the car, so keen were they to be the first to greet Annette. It was like a royal procession!

'Hoo lang are ye stayin', Annette?'

'Well, it's fine tae see ye, hinny! Hoo are ye keepin'?'

'Hoo's Lunnon, an' the dancin', Miss Annette?'

'Yer's no' a bit fatter, Annette hinny! Ye still look a bit bairn!'

'Do I?' laughed Annette, loving their warm Northumbrian voices. 'Well, I expect it's a good thing, since I'm a dancer. Most dancers are terrified of getting fat . . . Oh, no, Martha, I'm not staying for all that long. As a matter of fact I'm really only staying for a full day, and that's tomorrow, Christmas Day. I have to be off again at crack of dawn on Boxing Day.

Angus and his father are taking me in to catch the morning train. You see, we open at the Cosmopolitan Theatre in the evening, and I'm understudying the principal dancer in the ballet . . . Oh, yes, of course it's worth it, even for just one whole day. It's worth anything to see Dancing Peel again, and Mintlaw, and all of *you*. Besides there's most of today left and I'm coming to the hop, and there's the Midnight Mass. Of course it's worth it . . . '

It was the hop of hops! Never had so many people crowded into the little village hall! First there were games for the 'bairns'; then a short one-act play by the Women's Institute, and after this came the moment everyone was waiting for – the moment when Annette danced for them. She danced several of the Fairy Variations from *The Sleeping Beauty*. First the Fairy of the Crystal Fountain, wearing a little jewelled crown like frozen dewdrops, then the Fairy of the Enchanted Garden. After this came the Fairy of the Songbirds, with delicate fluttering hands, and last of all the famous Lilac Fairy Variation. Angus, watching from the back of the hall, thought this last dance the most beautiful of all. It was so dreamy and unearthly that you could almost smell the double white lilac, drenched with dew, filling the garden with its heady fragrance.

When Annette had gone away to change into her everyday clothes, the hop itself began. The evening took the form of a barn dance, familiar to all Northumbrians, the evening being given over, for the most part, to the good old Border and Scottish dances.

At the end of the third reel of the evening the vicar held up his hand and quietness fell upon the hall. It was a quarter to twelve and time to set off for the Christmas Mass. In a few minutes they were trooping across to the church, whose windows were now all lit up. The moon was setting behind a bank of cloud but the stars illuminated the snowy ground so that it was light enough to see. A laughing crowd of carol-singers had collected in the porch, ready to sing yet more carols in their own tiny church. It had grown cold – so cold that you could hear a faint 'singing' in the air, which meant that the thermometer stood below zero.

Inside the church all was warm and cheerful. The big stoves had been on all day, and gusts of hot air came up through the gratings in the flagged floor. Candlelight flickered everywhere and a delicate candelabrum, loaded with candles, hung in the chancel like a jewel. The worshippers, many of them from moorland homes miles away, brought their storm-lanterns into the church with them and hung them on hooks at the ends of the pews, and so added to the mellow light. Branches of holly, its red berries shining against the dark-green polished leaves, lay on the broad stone window-ledges. The font was covered by Christmas roses, brought from the Coldburn gardens, and a Christmas tree, decorated by the children themselves, stood proudly in the Children's Corner together with a crib. Pale lilies gleamed

on the altar, and the pulpit was a mass of bronze chrysanthemums – everyone had had a hand in the decorations.

When they came out of the service the moon had set but it was still light because of the covering of snow upon the ground. Angus and Annette stood for some time wishing their friends a merry Christmas, then they went back to the peel-tower for a cup of hot chocolate and sandwiches before going to bed. As they stood in the Round Lounge they could see through a narrow little window by the fireplace which looked out into the old kitchen, and thence through a slit in the wall that surrounded the peel, the bobbing, twinkling lights of the torches and lanterns of the worshippers as they went home along the well-known tracks over the lonely moorland.

'Goodnight, Annette,' said Angus, after they had drunk their chocolate and were standing in the hall. 'I am wishing you a very happy Christmas.' His soft Highland voice suddenly became stilted. 'I well remember making you a promise, Annette, that I do not mean to break – not in the ordinary way. But you see – you are standing right beneath the mistletoe . . .' He stooped and kissed her.

'Good gracious, so I am!' laughed Annette. 'Oh, well – mistletoe doesn't count, does it?'

Angus didn't reply, but stood watching her as she disappeared up the little twisting staircase. *She* might not think it counted, but he had other ideas. *'A'chiall mo chridhe! Mo ghradh!'* he added softly. And if you do not understand the Gaelic, you will just have to guess what he meant.

8 CHRISTMAS DAY

Annette got up late next morning. Mrs Dancy saw how tired her daughter was so, in spite of Annette's plea to 'Call me early, Mummy, please, so that I shan't miss a minute of it', she did not knock on the door of the little north room until nearly ten o'clock. Annette had only just time to swallow her breakfast and dash off to church. There were not so many people at Morning Service as there had been the night before at the Midnight Mass, because many of them had to stay at home and cook the Christmas lunch, but in spite of this there was still a goodly crowd. Annette had still more of her friends to greet before going back to the peel with her mother. Angus and his father came too, for they were all having their Christmas lunch together. There was turkey with all the trimmings, and a large plum-pudding, and of course all the usual things to follow – candied fruit, nuts, almonds, raisins and chocolates.

'Oh, think of my figure!' cried Annette, waving them away. 'I shall have none left.'

'Or perhaps you may have too much!' said Mr MacCrimmon drily.

After lunch there was the ceremony of the Christmas tree. Angus and Annette had chopped it down and dragged it in from the wood the day before and decorated it with all the baubles and toys Annette had known and loved as a child. On the very top was a star made of tinsel, and below that an angel with outspread wings made all of spun glass. There were many other toys, balls and ornaments, and finally a host of twinkling fairy lights. Lastly the branches themselves were hung with tinsel and 'icicles', and scattered with 'frost'.

Round the bottom of the tree were piled all the presents, and Angus was at once elected to be master of ceremonies, whose task it was to give out the gifts, allowing a certain interval between each one so that the recipient would have time to unwrap and admire and thank the giver. There were presents for everyone – no one had been forgotten, not even Rob Roy the Dancy cat! For him there was a little grey mouse – not a real one, of course, but a stuffed one. The stuffing was of certain herbs that all cats adore, and Rob Roy could soon be heard all over the peel, throwing his Christmas present up into the air and pouncing upon it! Annette had done wonders with her pocket money, and had managed to buy them all something. For Angus and his father there were linen handkerchiefs with their respective initials embroidered upon the corners. Between rehearsals she had knitted a scarf for her mother, and a pair of woolly gloves for Bella, who pronounced them 'fine to keep the cald oot'. Mrs Dancy had knitted her daughter a ballet cardigan in angora wool, soft and fluffy, and the vicar gave her a year's subscription for one of her favourite ballet magazines.

But Angus's present was the one Annette loved most. With infinite patience and loving care he had made her a calendar. Each month was illustrated by an enlarged photograph of Mintlaw and its surroundings, so that, all through the year, Annette would be

able to see her home in pictures. For January there was a photograph of the village with its sombre peel-tower and its little church, nestling in a fold of the snowy moorland. For February there was a sheltered corner of the garden with the first snowdrops just coming into bloom. For March there was a windy sky and the daffodils blowing under the churchyard wall. And so the pages turned, revealing one lovely view of the Border village after another. For May there was a picture of Sarah Dodd's ducks with very surprised expressions on their faces, as if they knew full well they had just had their photographs taken! For September there was a distant view of Peel Fell, with the dark mass of Kielder Forest in the foreground, and October had a picture of Witches' Wood, with a carpet of fallen beech leaves and one of Sarah Dodd's cows looking over the dyke. Finally, on the very last page, which was of course December, there was a picture of them all – Mrs Dancy, the vicar, Bella, and Angus himself, with a crowd of villagers at the back. When Annette was sitting alone in her little room in London, she would never tire of picking out their well-known and much-loved faces.

'You *couldn't* have given me anything I liked half as much,' she told Angus, her eyes soft and shining. 'I adore every page of it!'

When all the presents had been given out and exclaimed over, Angus announced that he and Annette were going out riding.

'Riding?' echoed Annette doubtfully. 'Oh, I don't

think . . . ' She was about to say, 'I don't think I like horses very much,' but then she remembered that if it had not been for a gentle little Shetland pony, who had carried her patiently on her back through a storm all round the shores of Loch Hourn, she would never have had the chance of dancing in a film, so she hastily changed to, 'I don't think I'm very good at riding.'

'Och, but you will ride Sheena's wee pony, Morag,' insisted Angus. 'She will carry you fine. She is as quiet as a lamb.' He did not tell her that for the past week he had been exercising the pony so that it would be quiet for her to ride.

'Yes – but lambs aren't awfully quiet animals, are they?' objected Annette. 'They jump and bound about a frightful amount! If Sheena's pony –'

'You need not be afraid,' Angus assured her. 'Morag will behave beautifully, I promise you. She is as quiet as – as a little mouse. Will that do for you?'

'W-ell, I might just try a very little ride,' said Annette cautiously.

Eventually they rode right up to Ravens' Eyrie, and Annette found that she could manage Morag very well indeed and that she enjoyed riding after all. They could do no more than walk and trot their ponies because of the hard going, and this suited Annette perfectly. The fine, powdery snow flew up in a cloud under the ponies' hoofs, and each frond of bracken and sprig of dead heather was a diamond spray. The air was so cold that their breath came in white puffs. From the height of the hill they sat looking down at the miles and miles of tumbled moorland which the snow had transformed into a white eiderdown quilt.

'And now you will be telling me,' said Angus in his soft lilting voice, 'how it is that a Northumbrian lassie like yourself is afraid of horses.'

Annette had never before told anybody her secret – not even her mother – but now she told Angus about George, the blacksmith's son, and the birthday treat that had ended in disaster.

'Of course it wasn't George's fault,' she explained. 'Poor George thought he was being kind, giving me a ride on his pony, and he picked me out of the burn in a jiffy, but ever since then I've hated – no, I think the right word is feared – horses.'

'And now?' queried Angus.

'Oh, I'm quite changing my mind,' confessed Annette. 'I think they're lambs, after all. Well, no – not lambs,' she corrected herself, remembering what she had said about lambs. 'I think they're darlings. This one is, anyway.' She patted Morag's gleaming chestnut neck. 'And the dear little Shetland one that carried me all that way in Scotland. I shall never forget her.'

As they rode back down the hill Angus pointed out the fact that the sheep were all huddled together, with their backs to the north, and that the sky had changed from blue to a leaden-grey colour.

'I do not like the look of that,' he said. 'The sheep know that bad weather is coming, and the sky looks full of snow.'

The hills had suddenly become very cold and grey and, with a shiver, Annette turned her pony and trotted off down the heathery hillside in the direction of home, Angus close behind her.

'Oh, and here is the very hedge I was jumping when you unseated me!' laughed Angus. 'I well remember how I almost beat you with my riding-crop upon that occasion!'

'Yes, I was frightened to death,' admitted Annette, 'but of course I wouldn't show it! And there's the old cowshed where you locked me in. You didn't know me as well in those days, Angus MacCrimmon, as you do now! You might have known I'd get out somehow, though how I managed to squeeze through *that* – ' she pointed at the narrow loophole window '– I don't know. I must have been even slimmer than I am now!' A sudden awful thought struck her. 'Oh, Angus,' she added, 'you don't think I'm getting fat, do you?'

'About as fat as a darning-needle!' laughed Angus.

'You know,' said Annette, as they crossed the last field, 'I think it's grown warmer, or perhaps it's just that we have our backs to the wind.'

'Yes, perhaps,' said Angus, but he did not sound altogether convinced. When they reached the peel a few flakes of snow had already begun to fall.

There was a carol service that evening, and when they came out it was snowing in earnest. In fact there were already several centimetres upon the ground and drifts were forming. The wind was rising and blowing in icy gusts round the corner of the churchyard wall.

After they had had supper Annette and Angus offered to wash the dishes, since Bella had long since gone home, and was now celebrating Christmas in the bosom of her own family in the village.

'Angus,' said Annette, stopping in the act of drying a plate.

'Yes, Annette?'

'Do you think we're going to be snowed-up?'

'I was just asking myself that question,' answered Angus. 'I am thinking it might be as well if we were to get you into Newcastle tonight and did not wait until the morning.'

They went to the door and looked out. Already the snow lay deep upon the great rough block of stone

that did duty for a step, and was driving in an ever-thickening cloud against the lintel. With sinking hearts they turned back to the cosy kitchen. Through the narrow look-out window they could see into the Round Lounge. The vicar was sitting in an easy chair, toasting his feet in front of the roaring log fire. Annette's mother was pouring out the coffee. Martha Keenleside, who had come in for the evening, was handing a cup to the vicar.

'Oh, Angus – I couldn't, I simply *couldn't* ask your father to drive me into town tonight,' cried Annette. 'He looks so comfortable, and he's had such a busy day, poor lamb. Besides, he's such a dear!'

Angus smiled to himself. Annette was always saying these funny things without having the least notion that they were funny. This was one of the things he loved about her. Many young men fall in love with a girl, perhaps because she is pretty, or dances beautifully, or happens to be wearing a becoming dress. But Angus loved Annette at all times, and especially did he love her if she was cold and wet – yes, even when she had a red nose! He loved the way she did everything in a headlong rush, and the way the words spilled out of her wide, generous mouth so fast that they tripped over themselves and sometimes didn't make sense – or the sense wasn't in the least what she intended. He loved her straight black hair and her fringe, and her sad dark eyes, much too large for her little sallow face. He loved the way she walked as if she was blown by the wind and the gestures she made with her delicate, thin little hands. In fact he loved everything about her – her faults, as well as her virtues. It will be seen that Angus's love was not merely a passing fancy but the kind that lasts.

'I will tell you what it is that we are doing,' he said, looking down at her. 'I am driving you into town myself. Oh, yes, I can do so quite well. I am very experienced with the car. I will go and get it out now and you shall pack your clothes. We shall not tell them until we are quite ready. That will save argument!'

'But are you sure, Angus?' said Annette doubtfully.

'Quite sure, *mo chridhe*,' smiled Angus. 'Away with you now!'

And so, up in her cold little room, Annette packed the case that she had unpacked only a few hours ago. In the bottom – laid flat, so that it shouldn't get crushed – she put her precious calendar, and on top she placed all her other presents. The snowflakes drove against the north window with a soft hissing sound, like the rustle of a silken dress, and the wind keened in the chimney. Annette's eyes filled with tears and they fell hotly into the open case. How she hated to go! What would she give to be able to stay here in her beloved Border home with her mother and all her friends! But this could not be. The other side of her nature, the artistic side inherited from her French father, said, 'No, Annette Dancy. You must go to London. Are you not in love with the ballet? Are you not a little dancer?'

'Oh!' cried Annette through her tears. 'I don't know what I am! I'm torn in two!'

'A little dancer!' moaned the wind in the chimney. 'You're – a – little – dancer! You're like Hans Andersen's Karen. You dance because you must! Come, pack up your things and begone!'

9 BLIZZARD!

To you who live in a town, it might not seem such a great adventure to travel in a car from Mintlaw to Newcastle, a mere thirty-five miles, in a snowstorm. But imagine a lonely white ribbon of road, utterly deserted, stretching endlessly ahead, first over the moorland, then through patches of fir- and larch-trees, whose branches, already heavy with snow, make a roof across the road so that you dive into a tunnel, to be met, when you emerge, by a blinding white curtain of snowflakes. Since there was no heater in the old car the windscreen began to freeze over, and Angus had to stop every few minutes to clear a patch of glass by breathing upon it, so that he could see to drive. As for Annette, she couldn't see out at all. In front of her was nothing but an ever-thickening blanket of snow.

The strange thing was that, as they drove eastwards the snow grew thicker, the wind stronger, until there was no doubt about it – they were in the midst of a blizzard. Evidently the wind was blowing directly from the east instead of from the north or the north-east, as is generally the case in Northumberland, so that the nearer they drew to the coast the heavier and the thicker the snow became. Drifts had formed on the high parts of the road and at exposed corners, and they had to get out of the car and clear a path through them with a long-handled shovel. Fortunately Angus had had the foresight to put a couple of these in the boot of the car, together with a pile of sacks, just in case they stuck on a hill. As they drew near to Newcastle a strange sight met their eyes. All along the sides of the road were white humps, which turned out to be cars which their owners had abandoned. They were finding it hard to get along themselves – what with the windscreen freezing, the wheels slipping and the ever-deepening snow. There was now quite thirty centimetres on the level, and it was plain that here in Newcastle it had been snowing for several hours – if not all day!

Slowly, and with infinite caution because he could only see a metre or two in front of him, Angus drove to the suburb where Annette's Aunt Molly lived. He kept to the main road, not daring to risk taking short cuts which were badly lit and where it would be all too easy to have a head-on collision with someone coming in the opposite direction. But as a matter of fact, Newcastle was like a city of the dead. Since it was Christmas Night nothing had been done to clear the snow away. It covered the streets of the grey industrial city with a dazzling white carpet and transformed the grimy buildings into glittering palaces. Tomorrow the snowploughs would get to work, but tonight Newcastle was a fairy city. Angus and Annette, now that they were safely here, were entranced. At least Annette would have been if she hadn't been so cold; but having sat for the best part of three hours in an unheated car her teeth were chattering, and her face pinched and blue. Even the thick rug that Angus had tucked round her hadn't kept her warm.

At length they reached Aunt Molly's flat and Angus drew up. Whether he was on the road or the pavement he hadn't the least idea, for the snow had made them level, and no kerbstone could be seen. He got out, went round to the far door, opened it and helped Annette out. They were both stiff with the cold and with sitting so long in the car.

'There's no light in the window,' Annette said, looking up at Aunt Molly's flat anxiously. 'She may be away. We never thought of that. What will we do if she's not here?'

'Let's not cross our bridges before we come to them,' said Angus with an assurance he did not feel. 'She may be at the back, in the kitchen or somewhere. But of course – how stupid of us! – she'll be in bed.'

'Oh, no,' said Annette, 'there's only a gas cooker in the kitchen. Aunt Molly never sits out there, and she never goes to bed till after midnight and then she reads for hours. I have an awful what's-its-name –

pre-something – that she's not here. Oh, Angus, whatever shall we do?'

They rang the bell and knocked, but there was no reply, no comforting light was switched on, as would surely have been the case if Aunt Molly had been in the flat – even in bed. It was all too plain, the flat was empty.

'I suppose you don't know where she keeps her key?' said Angus at length. 'I mean, people usually leave their keys under the doormat, or under a stone, or somewhere.'

'Not in towns,' said Annette. 'They don't have doormats or stones in towns. They – I mean the mats – are inside.'

It was all too true. Aunt Molly's flat presented a porchless, matless exterior, and there was no garden, with or without stones, where a key might be hidden.

'Well, there's only one thing for it,' said Angus after a while. 'I suppose we daren't knock up the other people – ' he looked up at the row of black windows '– at this time of night?' He glanced at his wristwatch by the light of the streetlamp. 'Good lord! It's a quarter to one! We must go to the Central Station and sleep in the waiting-room.'

'That's all very well for me,' said Annette. 'I've got a ticket, so they won't turn me out. But they won't let *you* stay, Angus, because you haven't got one.'

'They might do so under the circumstances,' said Angus. 'Anyway, I can always sleep in the car. I'll be all right. The main thing is to get you fixed up, Annette.'

They got back into the car and he turned the ignition key. Nothing happened. After a few minutes the lights began to fade.

'The battery!' cried Angus. 'With having to drive so slowly it hasn't been charging. This car has a small one at any time. And that makes me wonder –' he flashed his electric torch on to the dashboard ' – yes, I thought as much – we're out of petrol! That's why she won't start. It's all that driving in bottom gear at fifteen miles an hour! It's amazing luck she conked out on Aunt Molly's very doorstep, but I suppose wherever we'd stopped in the last mile or so we shouldn't have been able to start again. Oh, well – that settles it, we shall just have to walk. It's obvious that there are no late buses running, and I don't know of an all-night petrol station round about here. It's lucky it's only a couple of miles.'

They set off down the Great North Road. Far above their heads the sodium streetlamps cast their unearthly light, making the two figures, with their yellow faces, look like visitors from another world! They stumbled along, Angus with his arm tightly through Annette's as he helped her along, and their heads bent low against the blizzard.

'Oh, let's stop for just a minute while I get my breath,' begged Annette, and together they crouched in the lee of a telephone box and shook the snow off their sodden garments.

'Hello!' said a deep voice. 'You two in any trouble?'
They looked up into the face of a burly police constable.
'Oh, yes,' said Annette. 'Indeed we are! At least poor Angus is.' She proceeded to pour into the ears of the sympathetic policeman the whole story. How she had come home to spend Christmas at Mintlaw, her part in the ballet in the children's play, the necessity of her catching the early morning train to London, the snowstorm . . .

'And now we've run out of petrol – at least the car has,' she ended up. 'So you see how it is, Inspector; I can sleep in the station waiting-room because I have a ticket, but poor Angus hasn't anywhere to lay his head because of Aunt Molly – Aunt Molly not being there, I should say.'

'The station waiting-room?' echoed the policeman. 'Pretty uncomfortable, eh? I have an idea worth two of that.' He took them, one on each arm, and piloted them straight to the police station, where they were received 'like royalty' as Annette said afterwards when she wrote to her mother.

We had supper in the super's room – hot soup and baked beans on toast. Oh, Mummy – it was such a thrill! Fancy sleeping in a cell! Of course the super gave me his own quilt, and fixed up a bedside lamp and an extra mattress. Oh, and a little bell too, so that if I wanted anything in the middle of the night I had only to ring and one of the nice policemen would come in a jiffy. Only of course I didn't – I was much *too tired. Still it was a real honest-to-goodness cell, with bars on the little window and on the door, and I was locked in (regulations, and so on). Think of it – how I shall be able to boast to all my friends! In the morning they brought me a cup of tea, and took Angus and me to the station in state – in a police van! The snow was far too thick for an ordinary car. It (the van, I mean) had bars on the window. We had a real police escort, too, to see us off! I shall never forget it. All those dear policemen!*

Well, now I'm back in London (actually I'm writing this in my dressing-room), and it's hard to believe that I've been home at all! But tonight, before I go to sleep, I shall look at Angus's calendar – the snowy photograph for January – and I'll be able to picture you all with the snowdrifts piled high against the dear old peel, and the moors with the violet shadows, and the village pump.

Goodnight, darling Mummy! I feel in another minute I shall cry – I miss you so much, and I'm so dreadfully homesick.

Your loving Annette.

When she had finished the letter Annette read it through, and then firmly crossed out the bits about feeling homesick so that they couldn't be read.

After all, she thought, it won't do *me* any good to upset poor Mummy, and I am glad to be back again – even if I am on the verge of tears. Oh, dear! How uncomfortable it is to be made in two halves! There's the Northumbrian part of me wanting to be back home in the north of England, and the French part of me wanting to dance. It makes it very awkward! She slipped the sheets of notepaper into an envelope and addressed it. Then she hummed the music of the Little Mermaid's first solo, and ran through the whole dance to make sure she had it perfect. One never knew what might happen!

10 NEW YEAR IN LONDON

During the next week Annette worked so hard that she had no time even to feel lonely. Every morning there was the usual class – ballet-dancers have to practise, even when they are dancing each night at the theatre. In the afternoons – when there wasn't a matinée – she was supposed to be free, but there was always the endless washing of tights, the darning and breaking-in of point-shoes and, of course, photographing sessions, though Annette had fewer of these than she would have done if she had been one of the principal dancers. Added to this, the school was already busy with rehearsals for the tour they were making in the Midlands directly after the close of the play. It was to be undertaken by the whole school, with the addition of Emma Gautier from the company as a 'stiffener', and they were to visit big cities like Manchester, Birmingham and Liverpool, among others.

It was fun to be dancing in one's own theatre, thought Annette, along with the company. It was a foretaste of the future when, at no very distant date, she would be a member of that company herself. Her training would be finished at the end of the summer, and, if she worked hard, Monsieur Georges had inferred that she would be accepted for the Cosmopolitan Ballet Company in the autumn. Sometimes, when she was all alone in her little room, Annette thought of that time when Angus and she had ridden through the storm so that she could take her RAD exam. And then, after all they had gone through, she had failed by one mark! She could remember the awful despair that had filled her; how she had thought that her dancing career was at an end, and that she would never, never be a member of *any* ballet company no matter how small and third-rate, let alone a company like the Georges Reinholt one, which, even if it was small, was very famous, and quite as first-rate as the Royal Ballet itself.

'I wouldn't have believed you if you'd told me,' said Annette aloud to the snapshot of her beloved Nellie Brandon, which she kept on her dressing-table.

Every night Annette arrived at the theatre in good time. Although she might be late for other appointments, she would have considered it a crime to be late for a ballet performance. In the long, narrow dressing-room, at a long, narrow table with make-up mirrors all down the middle, she took her place along with twenty or so other students. She made up her face with all the skill and patience of an artist, carefully covering her face and neck completely with foundation, rather as if she were preparing to do an oil painting, and then, with the greatest of care, blending in the rouge, and the shadows, and drawing in the lines which were to make her stage character. Her final appearance on stage, to anyone sitting in the auditorium, was as though she had no make-up on at all. You only thought how lovely she looked, and how different from most of the other members of the corps de ballet, with their too heavily rouged cheeks and made-up eyes. Monsieur Georges, watching critically from the stage box, nodded his head in approval. Yes, it was plain that the little one, his private name for Annette, had got the difficult art of make-up at her delicate fingertips! She would go far, would the little one, if only . . . Here a frown would crease Monsieur Georges's brow, for he had remembered the detested film studios. Supposing they got their clutches on Annette? And after all, what was more likely? His friend, Stanley Goldberg – there was no doubt at all but that Stan Goldberg saw in Annette Dancy just what Monsieur Georges saw himself, namely, an artiste in the making. A curse on all films, thought Monsieur Georges vehemently! For ordinary actors and actresses no doubt they were permissible, though never, in his eyes, desirable. For a little dancer – *non pas! 'Ça ne va pas!'* said Georges Reinholt Dutoit aloud to the empty box.

Although it is in Scotland that the New Year is celebrated with pomp and ceremony, it is also kept in

London to a lesser degree. The Cosmopolitan Ballet held a party on the stage after the evening performance. It was quite an occasion since, apart from seeing in the New Year, the company were also celebrating Madame Boccaccio's thirtieth year with them – first as a dancer and latterly as a ballet-mistress. The company had been called by a different name in those old days, and its headquarters had been in Paris, but it was the same company to all intents and purposes. To Annette as the youngest had fallen the privilege of presenting her with a bouquet.

Just before midnight the company went up to the flat roof, and stood there, huddled in coats and wraps, listening to the sounds which were bringing in the New Year. All over the great city clocks were

chiming. People in the street below were shouting and singing, and a far-off roar told of those who were doing the same in Oxford Circus, round the corner.

'Auld Lang Syne!' shouted Charles MacMillan, who felt his Scottish nationality keenly at this moment. So they all joined hands in a ring, and sang the old Scottish song that is sung on these occasions all over the world.

After the members of the company had gone back to the light and warmth of the theatre, Annette stayed where she was for a few moments, leaning against the grimy parapet. Above her was the dome of the sky, deep dark blue, mysterious, unfathomable. There were one or two stars in it – the same stars that at this very moment were looking down on her home at Mintlaw. She wondered what they were all doing: her mother, and Mr MacCrimmon the vicar, and all her friends. Were they thinking of her, just as she was of them? That's the best of New Year, thought Annette, it gives you a special time to think of each other! She wondered what Jaimie Gordon was doing, away up in Skye. He had been able, after all, to go home for Hogmanay, and Annette had asked him to give dear Mamie Slaughter and Deborah all her love, and Sheena too.

Annette didn't like or trust Sheena MacDonald, but she couldn't help being sorry for her. She couldn't remember her own father, who had died when she was still a small child, so her mother had taken the place of both parents, and sister as well.

Annette had no secrets from her mother – except tiny ones, like being homesick, and even then her mother guessed it, or the reason for her fear of horses. Into her mother's ears she poured all her hopes and fears, her joys and sorrows. She couldn't imagine what the world would be like without her beloved mother. And now Sheena's mother had been taken from her, and Sheena had no one of her own in the whole world to turn to.

'Oh, poor, poor Sheena!' Annette had said. 'Give her my love, Jaimie, please, and say I'm so sorry.'

'I will do so,' said Jaimie in his dignified English. 'I shall not be forgetting.' He was desperately sorry for Sheena himself, and anxious too. It was fortunate that he had not yet left Skye when Mrs MacDonald had died, so he had been at hand to help his ward. But he had had to leave her almost directly afterwards, and he wondered how she was managing all alone at Glendounie. Of course there were the Slaughters. Mamie had promised to do what she could to help the girl, and Jaimie well knew the generosity and kindness of the Slaughters, even if he sometimes smiled at their quaint language and ideas. Nevertheless he would be glad when his work on the film in London was at an end and he could go home for good. The filming in Skye itself held no terrors for him, or so he thought, for he would be on his own ground.

11 HOGMANAY IN SKYE

On the Island of Skye, at Airdrochan Castle, they are celebrating Hogmanay.

They are in the midst of a grand ball, and at midnight they have also all joined hands in a ring to sing 'Auld Lang Syne'. All the men are in full Highland evening dress, and the women wear tartan sashes, fastened with beautiful brooches of cairngorm and Celtic silver, draped over their bare shoulders. Only one of them looks sad and out of place. She is not wearing a ball-gown like the rest, but a plain black dress, which makes her pale face look even paler. Now they have broken up the ring and are dancing a Scottish reel – all except the girl in the black dress, and a dark-haired young man who stands beside her at the open fireplace, with its roaring fire of logs and driftwood. Now, if we want to know why Sheena is dressed like this, and why she and the laird of Airdrochnish are not dancing like the rest, we must go back in time a few hours – to the early evening.

Inside the castle all was warmth and light – Mamie Slaughter had seen to that! Six more heaters had found their way over the mountains from Fort William, and had been placed in strategic positions.

Mamie wandered through the rooms, and nodded her approval. They would do! She had even managed to get her own bedroom and Deborah's what she called 'really warm'.

It sure was a great idea to bring in the New Year by a grand ball, thought Mamie. All the folk who were anybodies in the island were coming. The MacLeods, the MacDonalds, the MacKinnons, the Campbells – all the lot! It never occurred to her to wonder *why* they were coming. Guileless Mamie Slaughter imagined they were coming because they wanted to; because they liked her as much as she liked them. The true reason was that, out of politeness, she had coupled Jaimie's name with her own and Pop's, and the aristocracy of Skye had accepted the invitation out of loyalty to the laird of Airdrochnish. All the Slaughters' dollars wouldn't have brought the Skye clans to Airdrochan Castle on this New Year's Eve, but the invitation card, with Jaimie's name upon it, brought them all.

Blissfully unconscious of these undercurrents, Mamie walked round the castle, casting an approving glance over the decorations. The great stone banqueting hall, with its pillars and its gallery above, where, later on, she understood, the laird's piper would play while the company dined, was a perfect picture, with its tartan hangings and branches of evergreens – the laird's suggestion. Mamie had added many pots of geraniums, also sent down from Fort William 'to brighten it up a bit'.

Upstairs, seventeen-year-old Deborah was putting on a wonderful ball-gown created by a world-famous French dress designer. With her usual generosity Deborah was lending an equally lovely gown to Sheena, who had no new dress. Mamie Slaughter's heart was full of pity for their motherless guest – so young to be left without parents. At the same time she did not understand the girl. A colder, more self-possessed young person than Sheena MacDonald she had never met. Not one single tear had she shed over the death of her mother. In fact she had seemed quite untouched. But what Mamie did not know was that Sheena had gone out, early on the morning of her mother's death, and run deep into the dim fir-woods that make a dusky ring round Glendounie House, and there, out of sight of the sympathetic eyes of Mairi and Eppie, she had lain with her face against the wet fir-needles and cried aloud in her agony.

'Mother! Mother!' she moaned. 'What's to become of me? What's to become of me?' She beat her head upon the ground, while the tears rolled down her cheeks. Yet when, after several hours, she returned to Glendounie House, she was dry-eyed, though her face was pitifully white. Here, at Airdrochan, she showed no signs of her grief. It was no wonder that kind-hearted demonstrative Mamie was puzzled. She wanted to throw her motherly arms round the girl and comfort her, but she dared not. She was far too much in awe of Sheena to take such a liberty! She would almost as soon have flung her arms round the laird of Airdrochnish himself!

Mamie opened the door of Deborah's bedroom and a cloud of warmth and French perfume met her. Deborah, a vision in an oyster satin dress with a fabulously wide skirt embroidered with sprays of golden mimosa, was fastening Sheena into a pale green gown, the hem of which was exquisitely worked with tiny crystal beads.

'The name of your dress is "Moonlight on the Water",' explained Deborah. 'Oh, didn't you know, they all have names – Marcel Manet's collection, I mean. He sure gets some cute ones! Mine is called "Breath of Spring". Simple but beautiful, don't you agree?'

Sheena nodded, thinking that the title fitted the wearer as well as the dress. There was no denying the fact that Deborah was beautiful – Sheena had to admit it. But simple! Never in her life had the Scots girl met anyone quite as simple as Deborah Slaughter. And come to think of it – she wasn't unlike a bit of mimosa herself: golden, and fluffy, and innocent.

When Deborah had fastened the last hook and eye, Sheena walked slowly over to the long cheval mirror – another acquisition of the Slaughter family – and stood for a few moments looking at herself. For the time her private grief was forgotten. She was very young, and the young do not stay sad for ever. Yes, she thought, she was very beautiful! The sea-green dress clung in all the right places, decided Sheena. It might have been made for her. It was, perhaps, a shade too low in front; she drew the silver scarf that went with it a little more round one slender white shoulder; but it certainly showed off to perfection her beautiful figure.

I must get downstairs before Jaimie sees me, she thought. She had a sudden flash of intuition that the laird, her newly appointed guardian, would not approve of the dress. He'd probably think she ought to be wearing a black one, and a subdued one at that. She said so to Deborah.

'Oh, but why, honey?' said the American girl. 'Sure, he'll think you look a picture!'

'Yes, but I suppose I really ought to be all in black,' said Sheena uneasily. 'My mother . . . ' A shadow passed over her face. 'It's only a few weeks ago, you know, since she died.'

'Sure, I know that, dear,' said Mamie Slaughter from the door, 'but it won't do your poor mom any good to have you going about looking like – like Lady Macbeth!'

Sheena said nothing. She wasn't going to argue with Mamie Slaughter, who would never – not if she lived in the Island of Skye for the rest of her life – understand the laird's point of view. Sheena herself understood it and, strange though it may seem, sympathised with it. She knew full well she ought not to wear the glittering ball-dress, yet she was going to do so. She simply couldn't resist it.

'I'll tell you what,' said Deborah, giving her hair a last pat, 'Momma and I'll go down and receive the guests, and then, when the coast is clear, I'll come back and give the okay to you, Sheena, and you can come on down.'

Unfortunately the first person Deborah met on her

way down to the great hall was the laird himself. He was quite unconscious of the splendid figure he made in his dress clothes, though not quite so unknowing of the fact that Deborah's young heart missed a beat when she beheld him. Indeed, he would have been particularly dense if he had not known it, for her admiration of him shone in her candid blue eyes. He stopped at once and asked her where Sheena was.

'Oh – I don't quite know,' stammered Deborah, blushing hotly, partly with guilt and partly because of Jaimie's glance. 'She's – upstairs, I guess. She'll be down any moment. Do come, Jaimie, the guests will be arriving any minute.' She tried to make her voice sound casual and unconcerned. She would have put her hand on the young man's arm to draw him away from the staircase, but she dared not. As she had once confessed to her mother when they were discussing the laird, 'I'm scared to bits of Jaimie Gordon, Momma – really I am. He's so dignified!'

Jaimie did not move, but stood looking down at her.

'What is it you are hiding from me, Deborah?' he demanded. 'Has Sheena done something wrong? That I can well believe!'

'Oh, no – not at all,' stammered poor Deborah, her heart going pit-a-pat.

'Well, I am thinking that I shall go and see for myself,' pronounced Jaimie. He offered Deborah his arm, which she took because she dared not refuse, and when he had led her to her mother he bowed and left her receiving the guests who were now beginning to arrive, while he himself went back to the staircase, taking the shallow treads three at a time. At the top, as bad luck would have it, he ran right into Sheena, who was waiting for Deborah's reappearance. For a moment they stood staring at each other in silence. Sheena had discarded her scarf when she had reached the top of the stairs, preparatory to making a dramatic entrance, and now she stood there with white shoulders gleaming, looking as beautiful as could be, but in Jaimie's eyes as shameless as any woman could be! Here was she, who ought to be in deepest mourning, her mother only just laid in the churchyard, exploiting her beauty! Standing there half naked, or so it seemed to the Scot, at the top of the stairs, about to make an exhibition of herself. Thank heaven he had seen her in time! He took her by the arm and led her, protesting, back along the corridors to her room, and shut the door behind them. What he said to her we shall never know, for it was all in the Gaelic, but this is the main gist of it:

'What is this folly? Do you not know, Sheena MacDonald, that to appear dressed in such a fashion will shame you for ever in the island? Where is your black dress?'

'I haven't got one,' said Sheena, with a toss of her head. She must brazen it out now! 'Unless you would have me appear in the dress I was wearing this morning.'

'Better that than to be a figure of scorn,' said Jaimie.

'But it is not a dance dress but a day dress with long sleeves.'

'That will not matter, since you will not be dancing,' said Jaimie. 'And neither, of course, shall I, out of respect to Caitriana MacDonald who was my friend. Come, now, be a good girl and change into your black dress. I will wait outside until you have done so, and we will go down together.'

'How dare you!' cried Sheena. She had caught sight of her beautiful reflection in the mirror and her heart cried within her. She raised her hand and struck the young man on the cheek, then stood back, afraid of what she had done. But Jaimie did not retaliate. He knew how overwrought she was, and, to do him justice, was truly grieved to be compelled to thwart

her. But when it was her reputation that was at stake, he felt he had no choice. Who knew better than Jaimie how tongues would wag in the island if his ward appeared in a low-cut, glittering green dress, only six short weeks after her mother's death! It would be useless to say she meant no harm. Sheena MacDonald's name would go down in Skye history as 'The Shameless One'.

'You must be dressed in *black*,' he repeated firmly, 'or you cannot appear at all. I shall be waiting for you.' He shut and locked the door on the outside. Then he walked to the end of the corridor and stood looking out at the silhouette of Blaven on the opposite shore.

When he had gone Sheena, too, ran to the window. Alas! This was not her home at Glendounie where, with the help of a thick mat of clinging ivy, she could have climbed down into the garden – even in a ball-dress. Below her window at Airdrochan Castle – thirty metres below – was the loch, with the waves seething and boiling on the rocks, for by now the wind had sprung up and the water was as rough as the open sea.

Strange to say, Sheena did not hate Jaimie for what he had done. In fact she felt vaguely relieved. He had saved her from herself. If he had not done what he had, she would at this moment be dancing in the green ball-dress and her reputation would be gone for ever! But of course Deborah and Mamie were both horrified, though Mamie herself wasn't surprised.

'Poor darling Sheena!' cried Deborah. 'I do think the laird is just too bad! However can you dance in that old black dress?'

'I am not going to dance,' said Sheena. 'I do not wish to – now. And neither will Jaimie. He told me so.'

'You mean,' said Deborah, with a catch in her breath, 'you mean that the laird isn't going to dance *at all*?'

'That is what he told me,' said Sheena.

Poor Deborah's face fell. It seemed that this Hogmanay dance wasn't going to be such a success after all. She had set her heart on dancing with the laird. She had, in fact, been trying all the evening to pluck up enough courage to ask him to teach her the eightsome reel, and now . . .

It's strange, but looking at the happy laughing crowd of merrymakers, with hands joined in a ring, all singing 'Should auld acquaintance be forgot' on the stroke of midnight, you might have thought they were all having the time of their lives, with not a care among them. And so it was with most of them but, for all that, there were sore hearts among them. There was Sheena in her black dress, watching the dancers wistfully but unable to join in; and Jaimie watching Sheena, wondering all the time what he could arrange for her while he was away in London for he did not feel it right for her to stay at Glendounie House alone; and Deborah watching the laird's dark, handsome face and wishing he would ask her to dance with him. Just one dance – that was all Deborah wanted.

All the young men had asked her except the only one she really wanted.

'You know, Momma,' she said later that night when the guests had gone and she had looked in to say goodnight to Mamie, 'I've fallen for the laird!' Deborah was like Annette and told her mother everything.

'You mean you've fallen in love with him?'

'I guess so,' said poor Deborah with a sigh. 'He just has to take my hand – to shake it, I mean – and I feel like as if I've had an electric shock, and when he talks in that slow strange voice – gosh! My heart just turns over! That means I'm in love, I guess.'

'I guess so,' said Mamie, 'but I hope not, honey.' It didn't suit her plans for her only daughter to wed a penniless Highland chieftain, even if he wasn't going to be penniless for much longer. In any case, the money he would make with his film was a mere raindrop compared with the ocean of the Slaughters' wealth. But money apart, Mamie didn't want to lose her darling Deborah, and that's what it would amount to, for she didn't picture herself living in this forgotten rainswept island for the rest of her life. All very well for a holiday, and for Pop's fish, but there *are* limits . . .

Part Two

1 ON LOCATION IN SKYE

The film *Pride o' the North* was to be a modern version of the Scottish ballet *La Sylphide*. There was to be a modern James, a climber nicknamed Pride o' the North, the part taken by Jaimie Gordon, and a modern Effie, his betrothed. She was to be a hard-bitten, knobbly-kneed hiker. No wonder James fell in love with a glamorous little ballet-dancer, who happened to be taking a holiday in Skye! There was to be a modern Gurn, James's best man, also, and it was he who was to marry Effie, leaving poor James forlorn – for of course, when it came to the point, the little ballet-dancer danced back to Covent Garden where she belonged! The fact that it turned out quite differently in the end certainly wasn't the fault of the script-writer, as you will hear.

The ballet sequences – *La Sylphide* – had been inserted in the middle of the film, making them part of James's dream – in fact, copying shamelessly the musical comedy *Oklahoma*. Although Annette supported the film loyally when she talked about it to her friends, she had to admit in her inmost heart that it was all very silly and artificial, with only the Scottish scenery and the ballet to recommend it.

Meanwhile the entire film unit: scriptwriters complete with miles of script, continuity-men, art directors – in fact everyone from the director downwards – had moved into the Youth Hostel at Glen Brittle. And now, much to Jaimie's and the local inhabitants' amazement, they had managed to haul their gear over the rough moorland into Coire Lagan, one of the most dramatic of all the dramatic corries of the Black Cuillin Hills of Skye. There, surrounded by a ring of majestic mountains – all over 900 metres high – they encamped by the shores of Loch Coire Lagan.

In his heart Jaimie, like Annette, hated it all. The very thought of this beautiful and remote corrie being taken over by a horde of scriptwriters, film producers and what-have-you, none of whom cared one jot for the beauty of the place they were working in, seemed like sacrilege to him. He would have taken no part in it had it not been for the dire needs of his village. But – facts must be faced – upon this silly film, not only his own future but the future of Airdrochan depended. In spite of his private feelings, he could not but admire the skill and daring of the cameramen as they hung at perilous angles, sometimes nearly upside down, over precipices and gullies, or halfway up glistening faces of rock, obtaining shots of the most hair-raising situations. Never would he forget the time they climbed up into the Great Stone Shoot of Sgurr Alasdair – 600 metres of loose scree! In that cold, echoing gully, filled with boiling mist and walled on either side by wet black crags, they shot one of the most spectacular scenes of the film – the rescue by Jaimie of Gurn from the belach between the peaks of Alasdair and Tearlach where he had fallen, injured. As he directed operations, with the injured man strapped to a stretcher, Jaimie marvelled at the amount of discomfort these film actors cheerfully endured for the sake of their art. Indeed his opinion of the film began to change a little at this point. It was to change a great deal more before very long!

Now it must be explained here that Meriel, the little ballet-dancer, was an expert climber. She had been specially chosen out of hundreds of actresses because of this ability. What did the film director care that all she could do in the dancing line was to part her hair in the middle and occasionally stand in fifth position! It was of course essential that Meriel should resemble Annette to some extent, and so she did – as far as her figure was concerned. She was the most fairylike creature imaginable, and Jaimie never ceased to wonder at the amazing strength and agility those fragile-seeming limbs possessed. It was as well, too, considering what was expected of her, and, to do her justice, she refused to employ a double.

By the end of May, a few weeks after their arrival, the film company was nearing the end of the climbing scenes, and all was now set for the grande finale – in other words, the thrilling ascent of the Inaccessible

Pinnacle of Sgurr Dearg by Jaimie and Meriel, with a spectacular rescue of Meriel by stretcher from the top. Up to now the weather had been perfect, as it so often is in the Western Highlands during May. But the night before the great climb it suddenly changed. The climbers, including Angus, who had obtained special leave from his school to take part, and members of the film unit who were camping in Coire Lagan, crawled out of their sleeping bags in the morning to find a cold wind sweeping down the corrie and the tops of the mountains hidden by swirling clouds of mist. It was not actually raining, however, and occasionally there was a break in the mist and a gleam of watery sunlight so it was decided to carry on shooting the scene. The effect, it was thought, would be even finer, though more difficult to achieve, than pictures shot in fine weather. So, the rest of the party having arrived from Glen Brittle, they set off for the slopes of Dearg, up which they must climb to reach the pinnacle, the climbers with their ropes and nailed boots, the cameramen with their gear.

It had been after long argument that they had finally decided upon the ascent of the Inaccessible Pinnacle by the south-west crack. They would, so Jaimie assured them, get unsurpassed shots of himself and Meriel clinging like flies to the thirty-metre crack. In few places would the climbers be wholly out of sight. Also, with thirty metres of rope firmly belayed round a spur of rock at the top of the crack, the safety of the two principal climbers would be assured. So the pinnacle it was, and there they all were, at the foot of a great face of rough red rock cleft from top to bottom by a vertical crack.

'This is the South Crack,' explained Bill, a knowledgeable hiker, who was staying at Glen Brittle Lodge, and who had joined the party in Coire Lagan mainly out of curiosity. 'It leads straight to the upper East Ridge. The East Ridge – ' he pointed away to the right '– is only thirty-five metres high, but all the same it's a real arête, and exposed too. The west ridge over there to the left is shorter and even more of a climb. The whole thing is awfully narrow, and the north face on the far side falls straight to the corrie. Do you see the dyke of basalt halfway up? It forces the climber right out of the crack and he has to swing outwards on his hands to get a foothold on the dyke itself. Of course they'll do it today with a rope from above. Lucky there's a north wind, so they'll be sheltered.'

The cameramen listened to all this with growing excitement, but Jaimie said nothing. Presently he asked Angus to take a rope up the 'easy' east ridge as far as the top of the crack and Angus did so, taking in tow a couple of intrepid photographers. These he left at the top of a steep pitch, where the ridge, which had narrowed to a mere forty-five centimetres in width, flattened out somewhat, affording a convenient, if precarious, perch from which they could obtain some dizzy shots of Loch Coruisk, 900 metres below on the one side, and scarcely less dizzy, but quite as beautiful, pictures of Loch Brittle on the other. Or so Angus hoped, but unfortunately the weather was growing worse, and wisps of mist were now blowing over the mountain-top, obscuring the view below. But at least they would be able to shoot the climbers as they negotiated the dyke, being in fact about level with it.

The other cameramen, armed with telephoto lenses, stationed themselves as securely as they could on the screes some thirty-five metres from the base of the crack. At the foot of the pinnacle the rest of the party waited breathlessly for the excitement to begin. Presently a leg appeared over the skyline far above them, to be followed by Angus's head, well muffled in a balaclava helmet. He made several attempts to throw a rope down the crack, but each time it failed to clear the dyke. Eventually, however, one end of it arrived on the screes below. Jaimie said something to Meriel, who tied herself to the rope and began to climb slowly up the first few metres of the crack. Jaimie watched her intently from a short distance away and, after a word with the film director, he called her back.

'It is no good,' he said. 'Although the cleft is deeply cut, yet it does not hide the rope. We must make the climb without it.' He called up to Angus, and after a good deal of shouting the rope was hauled up. Jaimie then took a nylon rope from his rucksack and proceeded to tie-on, beckoning to Meriel to do the same.

Then he slowly began to climb – up and up – until he was just under the outward ledge of the dyke itself. Here he brought Meriel up to a narrow ledge where she belayed his rope over a knob of rock. After a glance to make sure the cameramen were at work, and grasping as far up the bulge as he could reach, Jaimie swung outwards on his arms with the effortless ease of the expert, drawing himself up until he was able to place a foot on the dyke itself and so gain entry to the upper crack. All this was done to a gasp of admiration from the onlookers below, while the photographers poised on the East Ridge nearly overbalanced with excitement! As can be imagined, all the photographers made the most of this scene and, so it turned out afterwards when they ran through the rushes, managed to get many exciting shots of both Jaimie and Meriel as, one after the other, they clung like flies to the rock face, whilst wisps of damp mist drifted past. Meriel's negotiation of the dyke brought forth a loud 'bravo!' from Angus, who added something in Gaelic for Jaimie's benefit.

'What's it like up there?' shouted the film director to Angus.

'Wind's fiendish!' came the reply. 'North side beginning to ice up. Top of Ghreadaidh's white already! It will make the rescue down the East Ridge look quite Alpine! Think I'd better get those chaps down so they'll be in the right spot.'

Angus wasn't sorry to leave his cold perch, literally astride the crack, and join the two photographers lower down. He tied each in turn to the end of his rope and let them scramble down as best they could, on a tight rope, to the easy rocks near the foot of the pinnacle.

'What a place!' remarked one of the men. 'Easy way up, indeed!'

Angus, meanwhile, scrambled back up the ridge to his point of vantage at the top of the crack, anxious to see how the two climbers were progressing. Despite the intense cold he was really enjoying himself! He found that Jaimie had already climbed about eight metres above the dyke, and was now preparing to bring Meriel up the place known as the 'delicate step', into the upper chimney. Angus wondered if Jaimie had decided yet exactly when and where the 'accident' was to take place, and was just thinking that the next pitch would be a good spot when, with the swiftness and horror of a nightmare, drama turned to tragedy. Jaimie heard a muffled exclamation below him and felt the rope tearing through his clutching hands, over his shoulder, off the belay, dragging him from his tiny holds. A burning pain seared his back as instinctively he braced his falling body against the walls of the chimney. In little over a second, but a second that seemed as long as an hour, he was safely wedged across the cleft and the fall was stopped. But Meriel's weight was still on the rope. She must have started to climb upwards without waiting for his signal and slipped from the 'delicate step' while he was adjusting the belay. Possibly the step was iced and this had caused the catastrophe. She must have shot out over the dyke and then crashed back against the vertical wall below. At this very moment she might well be hanging unconscious with the rope round her waist, gradually suffocating. Unless he could take her weight off the rope he could not himself move with safety. But there was Angus . . .

'*Don't move*! I'm abseiling down!' came Angus's voice. He had looped the thirty-metre rope near its mid-point round a convenient spike on the ridge and was already descending rapidly, with the doubled rope passing under one thigh and over the opposite shoulder, paying it out hand over hand as he came down. With difficulty he managed to pass Jaimie and was soon standing on the dyke itself.

'Meriel, are you all right?' he shouted, holding the doubled rope in one hand and leaning as far as he dared over the dyke. And then, with a gasp of relief, he saw her head, and at that moment she looked up and smiled wanly. It was clear that she could hardly speak.

In a moment Angus had eased the girl's weight from Jaimie, who found a stance lower down, bracing the rope against his body.

'Meriel! Catch hold of that ledge!' shouted Angus as he hauled on the rope. Meriel obeyed and was pulled breathless on to the dyke where she collapsed in a dead faint.

'Quick, Jaimie, we must loosen the rope!' shouted Angus. In a few moments Jaimie was by his side and together they retied Meriel firmly but so that she could breathe, and laid her down as comfortably as possible on the sloping top of the dyke.

Meanwhile much shouting was going on below, the film director feeling that he ought to be taking charge of the rescue operations but, now that it had turned into an all-too-real rescue, not knowing quite what to do. Jaimie peered over the edge of the slab and shouted to him:

'We must have the stretcher! Can you throw us another rope?'

But alas! It was too far and, try as they would,

they could not reach the dyke.

'All right – we'll cut this one . . . Nothing else to do. Must have three ropes.'

But Bill the knowledgeable hiker's sense of propriety was outraged. Cut a climbing rope, indeed! What an idea!

'I'll bring one round!' he yelled and, grabbing the nearest coil, he set off at a great pace down the screes to the foot of the East Ridge, thrilled to death to be taking part in a real rescue. Two photographers slipped quietly after him to mark his progress.

By this time Jaimie and Angus had loosened Meriel's clothing, and wrapped her up as best they could with their own jackets and pullovers. They had also managed to bind up her ankle, which was clearly broken, with scarves and bandages out of Jaimie's small rucksack. In a short time Bill had arrived at the top of the crack and let down the new rope, which Angus doubled and inserted into a loop made out of the second rope which still hung, doubled, from the ridge. He then dropped the ends over the dyke.

'Tie the loop to one end of the stretcher,' he yelled to the men down below, 'and the two ends of rope to the other.'

After some delay there was an answering shout of 'Haul!' and the stretcher quickly arrived at the dyke. And now began the business of tying Meriel to the stretcher. Owing to the confined space it was a difficult job, but eventually they managed it, and she was gently lowered to the eagerly waiting hands below. And now it only remained for Angus and Jaimie to abseil down from the dyke. Angus came first in fine style, but not so poor Jaimie whose hands were badly blistered from friction with the rope. Just as Angus was about to pull down the rope through the loop, a voice from far above yelled, 'Hi! Wait for me!' and a chastened Bill, encased in rime, came abseiling down from the upper ridge to the dyke, and then from the dyke to the screes. 'Gosh! It's awful up there now,' he said, shaking himself. 'I'd hardly dared to have risked the ridge alone. Was glad of your rope down! I'll help to carry the stretcher, shall I?' he added, with alacrity.

Meriel opened her eyes, saw Bill, smiled, and closed them again.

Buffeted by a rising wind they made their way painfully down the steep scree slopes to Coire Lagan, their boots grinding and crunching on the stones, and their breath coming in gasps and grunts. It was bitterly cold and it was hard to believe that this was the same place as the sunlit corrie they had been camping in during the last week. All this time Meriel, almost hidden under a pile of coats and sweaters, was asleep on the stretcher. It was a subdued party that wound its way round the dark little lochan, but gradually their spirits returned. After all, things weren't as bad as they might have been! As far as they could see, Meriel was only suffering from a broken ankle, whereas she might have been lying dead – and Jaimie beside her – at the foot of the Inaccessible

Pinnacle. Also, down in the corrie it was sheltered, though it had begun to snow gently. The cameramen were secretly wild with delight at having shot a real rescue, and could hardly keep quiet about it.

'Look!' said Angus, pointing to a number of white humps. 'Our tents! Let's hope the wind doesn't get at them and blow them away! Perhaps it's a good thing they're weighed down with snow, otherwise we might never see them again!'

And now they had left the corrie behind, and were plodding, mile after mile, over the vast stretch of boggy moor down to the hostel. They reached it just as darkness fell, and by now the snow had turned to

rain. Inside everything was warm and cheerful, and welcoming hands ministered first to the injured girl and then to the tired climbers and the almost exhausted but still cheerful cameramen. Meriel seemed little the worse in herself for the adventure, though her ankle was broken in more than one place. On the whole everyone agreed that it had been an exciting day.

During the evening Bill, who was spending the evening with the film party, for they considered him something of a hero, remarked to Meriel, with whom he seemed to be getting on very well, 'You know, you somehow remind me of a girl I once met in Portree. You aren't, by any chance, a dancer, are you?'

'Not exactly!' laughed Meriel. 'I'm just supposed to be one in the film, but Annette does all the real ballet.'

'Annette! That's her – the girl I mean! Her name was Annette. Never knew her other. She was dancing at the Skye Gathering Ball in Portree and she took the principal part in the ballet they were doing – *La Sylphide*.'

'Why, that's the ballet in our film!' exclaimed Meriel in astonishment. 'How very strange!'

But of course it wasn't as strange as they imagined, because it was at the Skye Gathering Ball that Stanley Goldberg had first seen Annette and had decided that this was the ballet he wanted to use in his film. As for Bill – we won't mention the number of times he went to see *Pride o' the North* when it was released to the general public, just for the sake of watching a little dancer who had captured his heart with her grace and charm. He liked watching Meriel too, both for her own sake and also because she resembled Annette.

Angus and Jaimie were glad to turn in that night. They had both begun to feel the after-effects of their adventure. As Angus climbed stiffly into his bunk, he remarked with a yawn, 'We mustn't forget to collect my rope. It's still up there, frozen fast to that spike! Bill said he tried to get it off but couldn't manage it. Gosh, Jaimie – what have you done to your back? It is all bleeding!'

'Och, it is only a scratch!' replied the laird of Airdrochnish.

2 SHEENA MEETS A STRANGER

When the anxiety about poor Meriel was over – the doctor summoned from Portree assured them that her ankle would be fit again in a mere six or seven weeks provided all went well and no complications set in – the film company found themselves on the horns of a dilemma. Must they alter the ending of the film – for how could poor Meriel, with her ankle broken in two places, possibly flit from Airdrochan Castle by moonlight, or indeed by any other means, as arranged? They could, of course, employ a double, but no one was in favour of this. Nor would cutting the last climbing scene solve the problem as it wouldn't restore Meriel to health and strength. Moreover, after seeing the rushes of the rescue of Meriel from the Inaccessible Pinnacle which, with great foresight, the cameramen had gone on filming, they all agreed it was by far the best part of the whole film. It was quite unthinkable to cut it out! Jaimie, sitting at the back of the darkened room they had rigged up at the hostel, saw the film with its silly story and artificial contrivings come to life before his very eyes. He forgot about the story, and only saw the grandeur of the mountains of Skye and the drama that was taking place on the topmost pinnacle of one of them.

'Well, there's only one thing to do,' said Len Murry, the assistant director, 'and that's to alter the ending. It was a gloomy ending anyway. Tell you what – ' to Harry Preston, the scriptwriter ' – how about making James marry his dancer after all? I expect he would in real life. Girls always marry the blokes who rescue them on mountains.'

'How do you know?' asked Harry curiously. 'Ever rescued one?'

'Who, *me*? Good lord no! Mountain rescue not in my line. But a bit of imagination, though! Girl lying there with broken ankle. Nothing to do but think of how she's been saved from a horrible death by her lover. Got a spark of gratitude, hasn't she? Of *course* she married the poor chap. I don't know why we didn't think of it before.'

'What about her career as a dancer?' demanded Harry, loath to change his script.

'Oh, *that*! Career at an end, and so forth,' pronounced Len airily. 'Let's have the jolly old fade-out at Meriel's bedside!'

And so it was arranged. In less time than it takes to tell, the film unit, complete with Meriel on a stretcher made out of two deckchairs lashed together, were back at Airdrochan Castle and busy with the last scene.

And talking about castles – where were the Slaughters in all this excitement? Surely Mamie Slaughter was in her element, with a film being made in her very dining-room? But truth to tell, the Slaughters had left Skye and gone to London just before Easter. Mamie, although she had, not so long ago, declared that wild horses wouldn't drive her away from Airdrochan Castle, now that a film was being made in it, had suddenly changed her mind and decided that she must 'take a look at' England. Nothing Pop could say about his fishing had been able to alter her decision. She repeated that she couldn't and wouldn't spend another summer in Skye. We, who overheard Deborah's confession to her mother on New Year's Eve, may perhaps guess why Mamie didn't want her beloved only daughter to pay any more holiday visits to Airdrochan Castle, but no one else had the slightest idea of the reason for Mamie's sudden change of plans. Mamie, you see, treated her daughter's confidences as such and told not a single soul of their shared secret. She was a strong believer in the policy of 'bringing young people together', was Mamie, and she blamed herself bitterly for what had occurred. She might have known what would happen with only the one young man – and he so good looking! – for Deborah to play around with. Darling Deb was bound to fall for him!

So in the early summer the Slaughters flew back to the United States. On the other side of the Atlantic they were met by Mamie's lifelong friend Miriam, accompanied by Dwight, her only son – a typical lean-hipped, sun-bronzed American of four and twenty.

'Why hello, honey!' he drawled when he beheld Deborah. 'Gosh, you've grown prettier than ever!' and he swept her right off her feet in a warm embrace, just as Mamie had known he would. And if, in Deborah's romantic young heart, there lurked the shadow of a dark-eyed, kilted Highlander with buckled shoes and a *sgian dubh* in his stocking, if she still heard echoes of a soft, lilting Gaelic voice, nevertheless she was overjoyed to see her old friend. Eighteen months later, when she was nineteen, she married Dwight and lived happily ever after, as the fairytales say, for, as a matter of fact, Dwight suited her a great deal better than Jaimie Gordon would ever have done.

But all this is in the future. It is still May in Skye, and the film unit has not yet given up possession of Jaimie's home, though to be sure they have come to their last metre of film and the fade-out has been pronounced perfect. All that remains is the clearing up. The cameras, the trucks, the lighting apparatus and all the rest of the paraphernalia has already gone and only a few last-minute things remain, and these are to be put aboard the steamer when it calls at Armadale next day.

To celebrate the successful conclusion of the film, the film personnel went in a body to Portree for a grand dinner-party at one of the big hotels, where they would stay for the night and be ready to catch the steamer on its way to Kyle of Lochalsh next morning. For transport they used one of the remaining trucks, together with Jaimie's brand-new car. Meriel was lifted carefully into this – though, as a matter of fact, she could hobble along quite well, since her leg was in plaster of Paris. She was looking remarkably fit, so perhaps the enforced rest had done her good!

Only one member of the party was left behind, a showy young man called Bob Bowman, the youngest and newest of the cameramen. Someone had to do the last-minute jobs, and so of course it fell to him. Poor Bob! No wonder he was disgruntled.

While the film was being made in his castle, Jaimie had taken good care to keep Sheena away from it all. No one knew better than he about what he called her insane longing to be a film star, and he was certainly not going to help her in that direction! Feeling that it was not right for her to live alone at Glendounie House, he had persuaded his cousin Mary to stay with his ward for a month or so. After this Sheena would be going on a long visit to Northumberland. Mrs Dancy, feeling sorry for the motherless girl, had asked her to stay at Dancing Peel during the school holidays. Angus would be there, and perhaps, though this was largely wishful thinking on Mrs Dancy's part, Annette as well.

Jaimie had told his cousin in confidence about Sheena's obsession, and had asked her to do what she could to keep the girl away from Airdrochan Castle for the next few weeks. And so it happened that Sheena knew nothing whatever about the film and had not seen anything of the people who were making it until she arrived unexpectedly at the castle on this their last day. To her amazement she found Morag MacLeod, who helped in the laird's kitchen, busily stripping beds.

'What?' exclaimed Sheena, after she had questioned Morag. 'You mean they've *finished* the film? But why was I not told of it?'

'I am not knowing,' said Morag, plumping up a feather bed and beating a pillow. 'Maybe the laird –'

'I can well believe that!' exclaimed Sheena in a passion. 'And now they are all gone – gone back to London?'

'Och, no. They iss only gone to Portree,' answered Morag, 'for a wee celebration. But tomorrow – could you not be helping me with the folding of the blankets, Miss Sheena? – tomorrow they iss going back to England. They are catching the steamer from Portree in the morning. It iss very sad!'

'And my guardian – has he gone to Portree too?' demanded Sheena, as she helped the woman to fold the blankets and pile them on the stripped beds.

'Och, yes, he iss gone too,' said Morag. 'There is only the one young man left – the one they call Bob. I feel sorry for that young man!'

'Bob?' repeated Sheena. 'Is he one of the film men?'

Even a young man with the unromantic name of Bob might be better than nothing. She could, perhaps, find out how you got into films from him.

'Yess – he iss one of the film men,' said Morag, picking up a mountain of sheets. 'He iss out on the terrace, I think. Poor young man!'

Sheena found Bob, as Morag had said, out on the terrace. He was leaning against the mossy parapet and gazing gloomily across the loch at the great mountain Blaven.

'Very nice,' said Bob sarcastically, 'I *don't* think! Not so bad with the other chaps about, but darned depressing when one's all by oneself. Too much of a good thing, if you ask me! Oh, well – jolly old London day after tomorrow, and will I be glad!' Bob, as can be seen, was not a lover of the beauties of nature.

And then he saw The Girl! He gave her capital

letters, because she was one of the prettiest girls he had ever seen – or perhaps it was because he hadn't seen many girls lately! Anyway she was what Bob called 'an eyeful'. She had tawny hair and grey-green eyes, and a slender lissom figure.

'Whew!' said Bob, whistling softly.

'Are you with the film people?' asked Sheena, well aware of the impression she had made upon him.

'Why, yes – I guess so,' said Bob. He went on to tell her about his work on the film and, from what he said, he might have been the film director himself. But there was no harm in him, and nobody was more dismayed than Bob at the consequences of his flowery story-telling.

'What I can't understand, baby,' said he, as Sheena came to his side, 'is why they haven't roped you in for this film. Why, you'd sure make it!'

'Oh, do you think so?' said Sheena eagerly. It's perilously easy to believe something you want, with all your heart, to believe. 'You really think I could be a film actress?'

'Yeah!' said Bob who, although born in London, affected an American accent for reasons best known to himself. Indeed he was far more American in his speech than most Americans themselves! 'I should say so!'

'I've always wanted to be in films,' said Sheena longingly. According to some of the romantic stories she read to relieve her loneliness, all was going according to plan. You were discovered by a young up-

and-coming film director like this young man here, and your career as a film star began!

'With your looks and personality that oughtn't to be difficult,' said Bob. 'They only have to *see* you in the studios and you'd be a wow!'

'Or maybe you could be a model,' he added, romancing as he went along. 'Clothes, you know, or strings of pearls, or, or – oh, there are a hundred and one things a girl like you could model. I have a girl friend who makes a fortune doing nothing but show off wedding gowns.'

'How wonderful!' exclaimed Sheena, her thoughts switching over from films to modelling – she'd always wanted to model clothes. 'Do you think I'm good-looking enough and have a good enough figure to be a model?'

'Do I *think*!' said Bob, casting up his eyes. 'I *know*! Why, honey, they've only got to *see* you and the job's yours. When you want to try your hand as a model just you apply to your Uncle Bob. He'll fix you up in no time.'

The Scots girl had no sense of humour. Nor was she used to people who said more than they meant. Most of her acquaintances meant a great deal more than they said. She took all Bob's blandishments and boasting statements as the plain truth. But of course you couldn't really blame Bob for this. He never imagined that any girl would take what he said seriously, so he was quite innocent in heart of what happened as a consequence of his boastful words.

'Let's have supper together, shall we?' said Sheena. 'I'll tell Morag and she'll cook us something. You don't know,' she added, 'how lonely I get, with only Mary Gordon – she's the laird's cousin, you know – to talk to. All she can talk about is the minister's sermon last Sunday, and how things aren't the same as they were when she was young. Of *course* they aren't! Things always change, don't they?'

'Sure!' said Bob.

After supper they went out on to the terrace again and Bob felt more kindly towards the mountain landscape. It wasn't so bad now that he had a pretty girl to keep him company! They said goodnight at ten o'clock, and Sheena went up to the little turret room where she usually slept and where Morag had made a bed up for her.

3 SHEENA HAS AN IDEA

It was quieter than ever at Airdrochan after the film people had gone. Blessedly quiet, thought Jaimie! He had not, so far, received any offers of more film work, but if he did he would know just how to deal with them! He could not imagine any sane person choosing to work in a town among crowds of people, all shouting and gesticulating and talking at one and the same time, when they could have *this*. His eyes took in the lovely prospect of sea and mountains afforded from Elgol, whence he had come in his new motor-launch to attend to a couple of sick ewes. Yet his work in the film had given him the money to buy this very launch, and a great many other things besides. When he had seen the state of his bank balance he had almost (but not quite) forgiven the film-makers for the four large sacks of rubbish he had collected up in Coire Lagan! He had marvelled that these shouting sweating technicians, with their modern paraphernalia of cameras and lamps, had left so little trace behind them. Much less trace, in fact, than those glaciers of long, long ago, whose scratches could still be seen upon the rocks around this lonely lochan. Just a few jars and tins and newspapers, and they were gone as if they had been a dream. Yes, passing strange, thought Jaimie!

Come to think of it, the same applied to his castle. Stripped of all the Slaughters' trimmings, it had lapsed, within a week of their departure, into the same austere old fortress that it had been when they had first taken it over. It would take more than the Slaughters to leave a mark on Airdrochan Castle!

Before he left the corrie Jaimie had looked up at the towering mountains that surrounded it. It was up there, he remembered, that young Angus MacCrimmon had lost his mother. She had been killed while negotiating the *mauvais pas* or 'bad step' between Sgumain and Alasdair. He had helped to bring down her dead body. Any ordinary person might wonder that Angus ever wished to climb a mountain again, but Jaimie did not. He understood, as would any other mountaineer, Angus's attitude. When you grappled with a mountain you first of all counted the cost and, if disaster befell you, it was through some fault of your own or your equipment – a broken rope, in this case. You did not blame the mountain.

As Jaimie rounded the tip of the peninsula of Strathaird on his way to Tascavaig to visit his ward, he pulled out of his pocket the letter he had received that morning from London. It was an invitation, printed in gold lettering upon thick white paper, to the world première of the new film, *Pride o' the North*. At first Jaimie had thought, Och, I have had enough of films, and decided not to go, when his eye had caught a postscript, written in Stanley Goldberg's sprawling handwriting, at the bottom of the card:

> *Royalty may be there, and it is likely that you will be presented, so put on your best bib and tucker, Jaimie my lad (by that I mean full Highland evening dress). Have sent an invite to the rest of the cast – including young Angus MacCrimmon and that pleasant hiker, Bill What's-his-name.*
>
> *Yrs, Stanley Goldberg.*

Jaimie then realised that the invitation was in the nature of a royal command, and that he would have to attend and in full Highland dress. For one brief moment he thought of telling Sheena about it, then decided not to do so. She might want to go, and already her head was too full of films and fanciful notions! He decided to tell her merely that he was going to London on business but he would keep quiet about the première. What she never knew, thought Jaimie, she would never miss!

He found Sheena in the garden of Glendounie House, gathering armfuls of rhododendrons. When he told her he was going to London for a few days her eyes shone.

'Can I come too? I've never seen London, you know, Jaimie. Do say I can.'

'You are knowing, surely, that it would not be fitting for you to come with me to London unaccompanied,' answered Jaimie sombrely.

'Well, couldn't Mary Gordon come too?' suggested Sheena.

'My cousin is over seventy years old,' answered Jaimie. 'She has never been to London, and I am sure has no wish to go there. It would be too much for her.'

'If it isn't conventional for me to go with you,' argued Sheena, 'I could go by myself.'

'That would be worse, if anything,' said Jaimie. 'You could not possibly stay at a London hotel by yourself.'

'Lots of girls do,' persisted Sheena. 'They go hiking and cycling, and they stay at Youth Hostels – '

'That is altogether different,' pronounced Jaimie. 'You are not one of them – you are Herself of Glendounie, now that your mother is dead. It is not fitting for the head of the house of Glendounie – the last of the MacDonalds of Glendounie – to stay at a hotel in London unaccompanied. It is not to be thought of, so let us hear no more of it.'

Sheena said no more. Most girls would have but Sheena knew Jaimie better than that. She knew it was no use arguing with him – it would only make him the more determined – but she did not forget or give up the idea.

To be fair to Jaimie, he did not realise that he was depriving his ward of anything worth the having. We know what his views on films were, and on towns also. If he thought anything, he considered that he was saving Sheena from her own folly. As for the film première – she knew nothing about that.

4 THE NEW BALLET

Since her brief holiday in Northumberland, Annette had been so busy that she had hardly known whether she was standing on her head or her heels. First of all there had been the children's play, *The Little Mermaid*. It had run for six weeks, and all the time she was not on stage Annette, who understudied the principal dancer, stood in the wings watching Emma Gautier as the Little Mermaid, and hoping that Emma would have an accident – just a tiny one, like a sprained ankle, or a dislocated toe would do, or perhaps a stiff neck! Even a stray germ of influenza, to keep her away from the theatre for a single matinée performance, would be better than nothing. But Emma had the constitution of an ox. Flu germs alighted on her very nose, then gave up the ghost and died! Her ankles, like her points, were strong as steel, and her toes also. No matter what draughts she sat in, her neck was impervious to them. Not a single performance did she miss during the whole six weeks, and the only time Annette danced the principal role was in the dressing-room before an admiring audience of corps de ballet. Once she stole down to the theatre when all the dancers had left and after persuading Charlie, who looked after the lighting switchboard, to switch on a few lights for her, she danced a large part of the ballet all by herself on the empty stage. Poor Annette! Where was her dancer's luck? It seemed to have deserted her altogether.

During the short tour that followed the play she was a little more fortunate. To be sure, Emma, as guest artiste, was given all the classical roles at evening performances – and at last nights, when all the bouquets were presented. But at matinées most of these roles fell to Annette, since, by her physique, she was more fitted for them than anybody else. Besides, she was so light that the male dancers liked to partner her. She had taken the trouble to learn how to breathe properly – to breathe in as she went up, and hold her breath until she came down. Also to spring as they lifted her, with the result that she was as light as a bit of thistledown, or a feather in her swan's headdress, as Charles MacMillan poetically put it after they had just come off-stage at the end of the *pas de deux* from *Swan Lake*, Act Two.

But now a most exciting thing had happened. Annette, Paddy, Marie, and several other students, had been told by Monsieur Georges that at the end of this term they would be taken into the Cosmopolitan Ballet Company. And as if this wasn't enough excitement, even more was to come. They all knew about the Cecchetti Casket? Of course they did! Why, it was the most important event of the ballet year for the schools – bar none! An anonymous admirer of the great Italian ballet-master, Cecchetti, had left in his will a sum of money and a magnificent silver casket to the memory of the Italian, to be competed for each year by all the ballet-schools. Each one must submit an original one-act ballet, the choreographer to be either a teacher or a student of the school, and this was to be danced by a team of not less than six dancers. Marks would be given not only for the actual dancing but also for the choreography, the décor, the costumes and the presentation.

Monsieur Georges had made up a beautiful little ballet, adapted freely from Hans Andersen's *The Little Matchgirl*, and the whole school was to dance in it and win the Casket for the Georges Reinholt ballet-school before they left to join the company. Monsieur Georges, wily as a fox, had not decided who was to dance the principal role of the Matchgirl. He picked out three girls – Paddy, Marie and Annette – and told them all to study the role and dance it in turns at rehearsals. Then, at the final dress-rehearsal, the ballet would be run through three times, the principal role being danced by each girl in turn. The company would be present, and as many VIPs as Monsieur Georges could persuade to come. He hoped to secure the presence of Oscar Devereux, the famous ballet critic, and perhaps also Sebastian Scott, the conductor, and his lovely wife, Veronica Weston, the ballerina. At the end of the presentations the appropriate principal dancers would appear before the curtain, and to the one who received the greatest applause would the coveted role fall. Should there be a dead heat, which would be most unlikely, for no audience is more critical than one composed of dancers themselves, the final decision would rest on Monsieur Georges.

Oh, the excitement that filled the ballet-school, for the decision affected not only the three girls but their three partners also. They had all learned to work, you see, with certain of the male dancers – Paddy with Phillip, Marie with Hans and Annette with Charles. Even the students who hadn't been chosen had their favourites. Feelings ran high in the school on the roof, and many were the heart-burnings and the speculations! Who would it be? Marie and Hans? They were, without doubt, the most vivacious couple, and the most advanced in technique. Or perhaps Paddy with her Irish charm and Phillip who had such wonderful elevation. But most people backed little Annette Dancy and Charles MacMillan. As for Monsieur Georges – if he had his own ideas as to who would be the Little Matchgirl, he kept them to himself. He knew only too well how to make his pupils work!

The excitement grew more and more intense as the weeks passed. You couldn't go into the big studio, except of course during class, without seeing someone trying out the difficult steps or *enchaînements*

Monsieur Georges had put into his new ballet. Of course they all knew the story well enough, but it may be interesting to note that Annette was the only one who got a copy of Hans Andersen's fairytales out of the library and took it home with her. She read the story of the Little Matchgirl night after night, until she knew it by heart.

As she read the story Annette saw in her imagination Monsieur Georges's ballet. The front of the stage was a snowy street lit by a single lamp. Snowflakes were falling, and now and then people huddled in greatcoats and mufflers passed by. None of them took any notice of a poor barefooted matchgirl, who held out her bundles of matches in her cold little hands, begging them to buy just one bundle. In despair the child, in order to warm herself, struck a match. Immediately the back of the stage was illuminated, and she was inside one of the houses through whose window she had looked so longingly. A table was laid for dinner, but the strange thing was that everything on it was alive – the goose, the knives and forks, the spoons, and even the dishes! The Little Matchgirl danced with each in turn before the light faded.

She lit another match! This time she was in another room. It was filled with children dancing round a Christmas tree which was laden with presents – dolls, toys of all sorts, gaily-coloured candles, and on the very top a beautiful fairy dressed all in glittering white. After a time the children, tired with their games, fell asleep, and the toys on the Christmas tree

came down and danced. The Little Matchgirl was entranced, and she danced with them all – even the candles! Then, just when she was enjoying herself, the light went out and she was back again in the street, with the snow falling on her long hair and covering her poor bare feet. Oh, how cold she was! In desperation she struck a whole bundle of matches, and at that very moment a bright star fell from the sky, which means, as you know, that a soul has flown up to God.

And now the scene was more beautiful than ever. The Little Matchgirl found herself on a snowy mountainside. Out of the fir-woods came a young man in glittering raiment. With him were snowflakes, whose crisp tutus sparkled with hoar-frost. They danced together, while the Little Matchgirl sat watching them in wonderment. And then the King of the Frost, for it was he, raised her up and, as he did so, her rags fell from her, leaving her in a beautiful white dress. To her joy she found she could dance more beautifully than any of them!

At this moment the backcloth lifted and beyond could be seen glimpses of Paradise – a sunlit land with fields of buttercups into which the Little Matchgirl danced, never again to feel cold or hunger.

The scene faded. It was morning, and the sound of bells filled the air for it was New Year's Day. In a doorway, half covered with snow, lay the body of the Little Matchgirl, and in her frozen hands she still held the burned-out bundle of matches. The passers-by shook their heads over her and wept.

'Look!' they said. 'She has been trying to warm herself! How very sad, poor little thing! And now she is dead. How very sad!'

Yes, they really thought she was dead, which just goes to show how stupid and earth-born the poor things were for, as we know, the Little Matchgirl had gone to Paradise and was safe with God.

Annette read the pathetic story so often that before long she felt she *was* the poor barefooted Matchgirl. But then it was always so with Annette – she dreamed herself into the role, whether it was an enchanted swan princess, or La Sylphide, the spirit of the Scottish woodlands, or a little mermaid who wanted an immortal soul.

5 THE TRANSFORMATION OF ANNETTE

Just inside the front door of the convent home was a little room called the office. Annette always paid a visit to the office on her way out, to see whether there was a letter for her from her mother or any of her friends in Northumberland. On one hot day at the beginning of June she found, lying on the table, a letter that was obviously not from her mother, or from any of her friends. It was in a thick typewritten envelope, and it bore a London postmark.

'Goodness!' said Annette absent-mindedly, 'I wonder who that's from?' She had been so busy of late that she had almost forgotten about the film she had made in the autumn. She did not connect the typewritten envelope with Unicorn Films Ltd. In fact she didn't connect it with anything at all. She slipped the letter into the right-hand pocket of her coat, the same old mackintosh with the same hole, still unmended, in the left-hand pocket, meaning to read it in the Tube, for she was late for her class.

But of course she forgot – her thoughts were on

other more important things, such as the *pas de trois* in the second scene, where she danced with the Knife and Fork. Something was wrong there. She thought it was John Fowler's fault – he lifted her too quickly, so that she came down too soon for the music. She would have to tell him about it – diplomatically, of course. Max would have been vastly amused if he had been able to hear her unspoken thoughts. He didn't consider that Annette had one jot of diplomacy in her whole makeup!

So engrossed was Annette in working out John Fowler's lift that she forgot all about her letter, and it lay there in her pocket, growing more and more grubby and crumpled, because of the number of strange things that were thrust on top of it.

It was by a mere accident that Annette discovered the letter at last – three days after it had arrived! Marie, the French student, burst into the dressing-room, throwing up her hands and exclaiming in a mixture of French and English, '*Mon dieu! Mon dieu!* But a thing of the most terrible as 'appen to me! I am lost! I am altogezzer ondone!'

Annette looked round. She was used by now to Marie's overstatements and divided all the French girl said by half.

'What's the matter, Marie?'

'Mattaire – mattaire! Et ees zat ze ribbon of my ballet-shoe is broke and zere ees no time to buy new. Ze *classe* ees in a leetle *quart d'heure*. Oh, *que faire*? *Que faire*?'

'Can't you mend it?' asked Annette.

'Ah, but you do not know, *ma chère* – you do not ondairstand! Ze needle and ze cotton – he ees not! I do not 'ave im, *non*!'

'Oh, well, if *that*'s all, I have a needle somewhere about, and some thread too,' said Annette. She could be very calm when it was someone else's difficulty. 'At least I *had* some. It was in the pocket of my mac. Just a minute, Marie . . . '

Out came the contents of Annette's pocket, including the letter.

'Goodness!' she cried. 'I'd forgotten all about that letter. I wonder who it's from?'

'L'aiguille!' begged Marie. 'The needle! Ze moments – zey are flying!'

'Oh, yes, of course.' Annette went back to her pocket. 'Here you are, Marie! I'm afraid the thread's green – does it matter?'

'Oh, ça va! Ça va!' declared the French girl. 'I seenk zat Monsieur Georges care more – much more – about ze security than ze *couleur*, yes! What 'ave you there, Annette, *chérie – un billet*, no?'

'You mean *yes*!' laughed Annette. 'Marie, your English is, as you would say, "a leetle of ze funnee"! Yes, I've got a letter. It's been in my pocket for days. I'd quite forgotten about it. Oh, *goodness*!'

'What ees ze mattaire? 'As someone die? Your face, she ees long as a wet Sunday!'

'No – it's my film,' explained Annette. 'You remember, Marie – the one I was in a bit ago? I'd nearly forgotten about it. Well, they're having a première or something, and this is an invitation. What an awful nuisance! I thought I'd finished with it.'

'Look out! You 'ave drop somesing!' cried Marie. '*Ma chère*, eet ees a cheque for five hundred pounds!'

'*What* did you say?' said Annette. 'A cheque for *how* much?'

'Five hundred pounds,' repeated Marie. '*Regardez!* See for yourself.'

'It must be a mistake,' said Annette. 'It just couldn't be true!'

But it was true, nevertheless. There it lay, on the dressing-room table, cheek by jowl with Annette's

tights and Marie's ballet-shoe, a piece of paper saying, *Pay Annette Dancy the sum of* FIVE HUNDRED POUNDS, and signed *Stanley Goldberg*.

By this time Marie and several other students who had come in to change for their class were craning over Annette's shoulder. The invitation card was identical with the one Jaimie had received, but the postscript was different. It said:

Since you are a very important young lady, and may possibly (though I don't promise, mind you!) be presented to Royalty, who is to grace our première, it would be nice if you were to wear a very special evening gown for the occasion. I enclose a cheque made out to you for five hundred pounds, and hope this will be enough. Don't worry, my dear – it will all go down as expenses!

'*Ciel!*' exclaimed Marie, expressing all their feelings. 'You certainly have the luck, *chérie*!'

'Five hundred pounds!' echoed Annette. 'And he "hopes it's enough"! How on earth could I ever spend all that on just one dress?'

'Ah, but zat ees most easy – *bien facile*,' said Marie, having recovered from the shock. 'Ze question ees not 'ow to spend five hundred pounds, but 'ow to get five hundred pounds in ze first place to spend! A dress, she cost fifty pounds – or five hundred pounds. Or sometimes, when she ees embroidered all over wiz leetle pearls, she cost five t'ousand pounds! Eet all depend. Me, I weel 'elp you to choose your dress, yes?'

'Oh, please, Marie,' answered Annette. 'That would be most awfully useful. You see, I've never in my life *had* an evening dress. Even if I'd had any money it wouldn't seem worth it, because I never go anywhere in the evenings. I'm always much too tired after the theatre.'

'But a world première,' put in Phyllida Dean in an awestricken voice. 'My dear, what a thrill! When is it to be?'

'Oh, I forgot to look at the date,' cried Annette. 'Let me see – it's – why, it's on the seventh of July! That's the day after the Cecchetti dress-rehearsal. What an escape! Imagine if it had been the same day!' Annette's face was tragic at the mere thought of what might have happened.

'But, *mignon*, eet ees *not* ze same day,' laughed Marie, 'Annette, *comme tu es drôle*! Est ees ze day after, so all goes well. *Ça va bien*, I t'ink. I go wiz you to a leetle shop zat I know, and togezzer we choose a dress of the most ravishing. *Non, non, non!* Not a made-ready! We 'ave 'er *made* especially for you. Ah, but what a dress! Zis ees on-ly on ze one condition 'owever, and zat ees zat I take you ondaire my feather.'

'Your *what*?' said the students. Usually they were able to guess what Marie meant, but this time they were at a loss. Then Annette laughed.

'She means under her wing, of course.'

'Wing – feather – *c'est tout la mème chose*, no? Yes?' said Marie with a pout. 'Your English language *est bien difficile*! *N'importe! Je veux dire* – I 'elp you to choose your dress on-ly eef you let me buy the underneaths also. Your underneaths, Annette, I 'ave see zem! Zey are veree funnee! Zey would make to laugh a cat! I ap-ologise, but eet ees ze truth, yes!'

Most girls would have been mortally offended at Marie's slur on her undies, but Annette wasn't. She thought too little about them herself!

'All right,' she promised, 'I'll let you buy my undies too. Is that all?'

'*Non! Non pas!*' said Marie firmly. 'There ees ze hairs.'

'My hair? What's the matter with it?' Annette put a hand up to the dark bush that ought to have been her crowning glory.

'Eet ees what ees *not* ze mattaire wiz eet,' said Marie. 'Oh, *là là*! *Vos cheveux* zey are like *un nid d'oiseau* – ze nest of a leetle bird, as you say. We must to find a French *coiffeur*. No one can cut ze hairs like a Frenchman.'

Marie was as good as her word. The very next day she conducted Annette to her 'little shop', guiding her gently but firmly past several large stores whose plate-glass windows were full of evening dresses.

'We do not weesh a ready-to-wear gown,' declared Marie. 'We will 'ave one zat ees made *on* you, *ma chère*.'

'Well, I do hope it isn't going to take too long,' said Annette anxiously. 'There's a rehearsal, you know – '

'*That* for the rehearsal!' cried Marie, snapping her fingers. 'Ze choosing of ze dress ees of ze most important. You must forget all ozzer t'ings.'

'Oh, dear – I'll try, but it's very awkward,' sighed Annette. 'You see, I promised Phillip – '

'*That* for Phillip!' exclaimed Marie, with another snap of her fingers. 'Ah, we arrive . . . *Bonjour, ma chère Lucile!* May I introduce Mademoiselle Annette d'Ancy . . . '

In swift French Marie explained to Madame Lucile about the film première, and the five hundred pounds, and how the dress must be beautiful enough to wear before royalty. Also that there must be the 'underneaths' to go with it, all in white satin and lace, and there must be an evening cloak 'for you cannot go to zis partee in zat old mackintosh, Annette, *chérie*!' made of velvet. 'And zere must be enough of ze monee left to buy *des souliers* – the slippers,' went on Marie, 'and al-so *un petit sac* – a leetle bag for ze evening.'

Together they worked out on paper the cost of Annette's outfit down to the last penny, while Annette herself waited, more or less patiently, and amused herself by trying on Madame's collection of model hats which, with her wild bush of hair, looked very odd indeed!

'And now,' pronounced Madame Lucile, after

some time had passed, 'zat we 'ave everyt'ing arrange', we weel proceed.' The two of them stripped Annette of her ancient skirt and jumper and began to walk round and round her, taking her measurements and discussing her good points and her bad with equal frankness, until she felt, as she said to Paddy afterwards, 'like a prize cow in a show ring, or a slave in an Eastern market being sold to an Arab chieftain for his harem!'

They draped a gleaming length of oyster satin round her, and immediately you could see the form of the dress appear, though as yet not a single stitch had been put in it. With a mouth full of pins, Madame Lucile went on talking – no mere pins could stop a Frenchwoman's chatter!

During the next two weeks Annette submitted patiently to three lengthy fittings – she who usually bought a new dress by pointing to the third on the rail and saying, 'I think that one will do – oh, my *size*? Thirty-four bust, thirty-four hips, and the waist doesn't matter, does it, because there's a belt . . . No, I won't bother to try it on, thank you. You see, I have a class . . .'

At the end of the second week Madame Lucile declared the dress to be almost finished.

'You call for 'er *mardi, oui*?' she said, as Annette zipped up her skirt and pulled on her jumper.

'Could you make it Monday, please?' begged Annette. 'You see, Tuesday is the dress-rehearsal of

The Little Matchgirl, so I just couldn't call on Tuesday.'

'*Eh bien, ma petite*,' smiled Madame. She had become quite fond of Annette. Like the good saleswoman she was, she had listened to all her customer's chatter about the new ballet and, like the Frenchwoman she was, she had become really interested in it. Who could fail to be interested, Madame would have said had you discussed it with her, when *la petite* was so all one way of the mind!

'And now,' said Marie, as they walked out of the dress shop, 'now we pay a leetle visit to my friend Anton, *le coiffeur*, who 'ave 'is shop in Meadow Street.'

'You don't mean to say, Marie, that we aren't finished *yet*?' cried poor Annette.

'Finished? But *non pas, ma chère*,' answered Marie. 'You could not wear zis so beau-ti-ful frock wiz ze hairs like ze nest of a bird! Truly, you must see zat! They must be cut. You must 'ave a shape.'

'A *shape*? Whatever do you mean?' As we have said, it wasn't often that Annette was puzzled by Marie's strange English, but she was now. Then a horrible thought struck her. 'You don't mean a wig, Marie?'

'A weeg? No, no, no!' Marie laughed so much that several people turned round and stared at her. 'You 'ave, I seenk, enough of ze hairs already wizout a weeg! I mean zat my friend Anton weel shape of ze hairs to make of you a new look.'

'Oh, you mean he will style my hair,' laughed Annette, with a sigh of relief. It was something, anyway, to know that Marie didn't insist upon her wearing a wig.

Anton turned out to be a sad-eyed little Frenchman with genius in his fingertips. The scissors in his hands were not mere scissors but the tool of an artist! When he had finished with Annette, it would have been hard to recognise in her the wild-haired girl of a short half-hour ago. On the floor, in a dusky semicircle, lay most of her crowning glory, and you could now see that she had a beautifully shaped little head.

After she had had a shampoo, and Anton had dried her hair, styling it with his pliant fingers, Annette couldn't believe her eyes. Why, she was – no, not pretty, her mouth and eyes were too big – but you might almost call her beautiful!

'Thank you! Thank you, Anton!' she exclaimed, flinging her arms round the little hairdresser, who, being French, wasn't as surprised as most hairdressers would have been. Neither, in fact, was Marie. Had such a transformation been made on her, she would have kissed him too!

'*Enchanté, mademoiselle, enchanté*,' he said, bowing to his customer. 'In a week from today – morning before the première – ' he had, of course, been told all about it, and about the ballet too '– you return, and I make of you so much beauty that you secure a film contract, yes!' Anton, of course, was joking, but his words were to prove only too true!

6 THE DRESS-REHEARSAL

The dress-rehearsal of *The Little Matchgirl* was held on the Tuesday afternoon at the Cosmopolitan Theatre. There were quite a number of people in the audience – members of the company who had been ordered to come by Monsieur Georges, and who dare not disobey, any more than they would have dared to ignore a royal command! But in any case, most of them wanted to come. It was at performances such as these that new dancers were first seen and appraised, and it was a good thing to know one's rivals! There were also many friends of the students, and friends of Monsieur Georges himself, and, last but not least, the Press.

In a stage box, well towards the back, sat an unobtrusive little man with a notebook – Oscar Devereux, the famous ballet critic. The hearts of the dancers fluttered when they saw him there, for they well knew that he could slay them with the sword of his pen! If they gained his approval, however, it was a real accolade. In a box opposite to him sat a dark young man – Sebastian Scott, the well-known conductor and pianist, and with him was his young wife, Veronica Weston, the ballerina. Monsieur Georges was in this box too, for it was well known that he thought a great deal of the young couple.

In an adjoining box sat a crowd of expectant young pressmen, cameras at the ready, notebooks in hand.

Sitting in the front row of the grand circle were two of Annette's friends whom we know – Angus and Jaimie. They had both arrived in London at the weekend, ready for the film première, so Annette had given them invitations to the rehearsal.

But now we must stop looking round the theatre for the curtain has risen. We are looking at a snowy street, lit by one lonely streetlamp, and in a doorway stands a poor matchgirl, holding out in her stiff, cold little hands her bundles of matches to the passers-by.

You might, perhaps, think it a tiring business to watch the same ballet danced three times over in the one afternoon, but you would be wrong. With each performance the ballet changed its character, as the respective ballerinas brought their very different personalities to bear upon it. So, anyway, thought Veronica, sitting in her box. Sebastian of course, was thinking more about the music, which had been specially written for the ballet by a young composer, Robert Wallis, one of Monsieur Georges's pupils.

The first ballerina was Paddy, who managed to infuse a little of her native Celtic sadness into the first scene. The result was that the Little Matchgirl was a sad, fey creature in the first part of the ballet, to be suddenly transformed into a bubbling, laughing dancer in the last scene. Paddy's roguish Irish beauty – black hair and blue eyes, with a pert turned-up nose – made one a little surprised that some of the passers-by, the young men, at any rate, didn't take pity upon so lovely a girl!

Then came Marie. The change in the ballet was unbelievable. It became sophisticated, like a stylised fairytale. The rags of the Matchgirl looked, on Marie, as if they had been designed by a famous French couturier, though they were in fact the same rags as worn by Paddy. It was impossible to believe in the first part of the ballet, but the brilliance of the second part was dazzling. Marie's crisp fouettés and pirouettes, her déboulés, so swift that she was like a top spinning across the stage, drew a gasp of admiration from the audience. The ballet, with Marie as principal dancer, was all in the grand manner!

And now it was Annette's turn. She changed into the costume that Marie held out without a word. She was no longer in the dressing-room with the other students; she had forgotten all about her friends sitting in the theatre, waiting for her to appear. She was in the middle of a Danish fairytale about a barefooted child who had been sent out by a cruel stepmother – Annette had imagined this pathetic detail, but no matter! – to sell matches . . .

'Oh, what a beautiful little girl!' cried Veronica softly. 'She's so pathetic she makes me want to cry!'

Annette, it is true, had none of the spectacular

brilliance of the French girl, nor had she the assurance of Paddy Dolan, but she brought to the last scene a tenderness and an unearthly beauty that made even the hardened Oscar Devereux's eyes grow misty.

The climax of the whole afternoon was, of course, the curtain calls, when the three ballerinas appeared to receive their merited applause. Paddy was received well, and Marie got some 'bravos' from onlookers in the upper tiers, but little Annette got an ovation. They clapped and they clapped! Annette was quite startled. Of course she knew she had danced well but she hadn't expected such applause as this. They wouldn't let her go! Monsieur Georges, hiding at the back of Veronica's box, nodded his head and smiled.

He'd known all along that the little one would triumph! As a matter of fact he'd written the ballet for her, though no one knew it but himself, so no wonder she danced it well!

Meanwhile, the curtain having gone down for the last time, Annette was receiving the congratulations of her friends backstage. Even Paddy and Marie were generous in their praise.

'Ah! No one could wiz you compete!' exclaimed Marie, throwing up her hands in a dramatic gesture. 'You were so beau-tiful! I, in ze wings, could 'ardly bear eet! Eet was so sad! I see eet now – ze last scene, he should be not of ze brilliant, but of ze tender!'

There were only two people who didn't join in the congratulations. One was Simonetta Delgarno, who hadn't got into the Royal Ballet as she had expected after all, and was still in the Cosmopolitan Ballet Company. She raised her eyebrows, as if to say, 'Why all the fuss?' She hadn't forgiven Annette for breaking into films. She had heard of course, all about the world première – Marie had seen to that – there was no love lost between the two of them! – and she was consumed with jealousy. The other was Pandora, who had never liked Annette anyway.

Without bothering to change out of her glittering white tutu, Annette sped by backways, along passages, up and down flights of stairs, until she emerged in the grand circle, not very far away from where Jaimie and Angus were sitting. They were in the middle of an argument as to whether or not they should go backstage. Angus thought yes, Jaimie emphatically no!

'I am thinking that it is not at all the proper thing,' Jaimie was saying, 'to call upon young ladies in their dressing-rooms.'

'Everybody does it,' laughed Angus, 'and anyway, I don't see how we can have a talk with her if we don't go behind.'

And then, suddenly, they beheld a vision of crisp white tarlatan, and there was Annette herself! The two young men got up, and Jaimie bowed ceremoniously to her.

'Good afternoon, Annette! We are enjoying your dancing a very great deal,' he said.

'Och, Annette – you did fine, lassie!' said Angus in broad Scots, and his eyes told her even more than his words.

That evening they went to Wembley to see some ice skating. Annette sat between the two young men and chattered away to them. Fortunately they were both content to let her do the talking. In the interval Angus disappeared, and came back with ice cream and a newspaper.

'There's a picture of you in it, Annette,' he said, 'and an article by that ballet critic – the one you told us about.'

Annette turned pale.

'Oscar Devereux? Oh – what does he say about me? Does he think I'm awful?'

'Read it for yourself,' said Angus with a smile, handing her the paper.

Leaving her ice cream to melt – for what was mere ice cream compared with the praise – or condemnation, of the great Oscar Devereux? – Annette skimmed down the paragraph. Then she read it through again more carefully.

> I watched with growing interest one of the students, Annette Dancy, who danced the principal role in the last of the three performances of this one-act ballet. Annette is very young and, of course, therefore lacking in experience, but she dances with a grace and insight far beyond her years. She has, in addition, the perfect physique for the classical dancer – long slim legs, softly rounded arms, small waist and hips, highly arched and elegant feet, small head beautifully set on graceful shoulders and an exceedingly expressive face. Besides all these attributes, she appears to be an

intelligent dancer (and, believe me, there are not too many of them!) and one possessing the gift of imagination. It was obvious to me that she had read and reread Hans Andersen's story, *The Little Matchgirl*, and realised that both brilliance and *élan* were out of place in this most pathetic of fairytales. Incidentally, this is a point which the two other competitors – Miss Dolan and Mlle Cocteau, both of whom danced with grace – would do well to note. Finally, although Annette Dancy is, as we have said, very young and inexperienced, yet I feel that she has great potentialities as a dancer.

I must explain here, for the benefit of the uninitiated, that this dress-rehearsal of Reinholt's new ballet was held prior to the competition, well known to all balletomanes, for the Cecchetti Casket. A great number of schools will be competing for this prize, and the Georges Reinholt School will be one of them. The competition, which lasts for one week, will take place in a fortnight's time (July 27th to August 3rd). Owing to the more or less secret nature of the original ballets presented, I cannot now criticise Reinholt's *Little Matchgirl*, but will look forward to doing so on a future occasion.

'Oh!' cried Annette, when she had read the paragraph. Then, to both Angus's and Jaimie's astonishment, she burst into tears.

'What's the matter?' asked Jaimie. 'Is it something that he has said?'

'Yes,' said Annette, blowing her nose. 'I mean, no! I mean he's said the most *wonderful* things about me! Oh, Mr Devereux – I do think you're a lovely man! Now I'm a *real* dancer!'

If Oscar Devereux could have heard her he would certainly have smiled. Not many people – if any – had called him 'a lovely man'!

7 SHEENA GOES TO LONDON

Jaimie had left Skye on the Saturday in order to catch the evening train to London from Inverness. When he had gone Sheena began to make her plans. She wondered what to do about Mary Gordon, who was still living with her at Glendounie House, but at the last moment the problem solved itself, as problems so often do. Mary received a phone call from Kyle of Lochalsh to say that her youngest daughter's baby had arrived sooner than was expected, and would Mary go at once to look after the rest of the family. So back Mary went on the steamer, feeling very anxious and guilty about leaving Sheena all alone, especially since Jaimie was away, but there was nothing she could do about it. She little knew how pleased Sheena was, or how the girl danced a Highland fling all by herself in the dairy after she had seen the old lady safely aboard the *Islander*.

During the weekend Sheena made her plans. She would ask Mairi's brother Donald to drive her to the quay. She would go on the steamer to Kyle, catch the train from there to connect with the evening train from Inverness and arrive at King's Cross in the early morning.

Everything went according to plan. Mairi and Eppie watched her curiously as she climbed into Donald's van with her suitcase, but were far too much in awe of their young mistress to question her doings.

'I am going to London,' she said, as she sat beside Donald, 'and I shall be travelling back with the laird.'

When the van had disappeared, Mairi and Eppie looked at each other.

'Well!' said Mairi. 'So it is to London Herself is going? I am wondering if Himself is knowing of it?'

'I am thinking the answer to that one is "no",' said Eppie. 'Well, as far as I am concerned, I am glad for the young mistress, but I am thinking it will be a good thing when Himself and Herself are married.'

Meanwhile Sheena and Donald were driving along the country road towards Tarscavaig, where they would take the road that cuts right across the peninsula of Sleat to Armadale on the east coast. Donald drove silently, while Sheena was far too busy with her own thoughts to make conversation. So they arrived at Armadale at one o'clock, just in time to see the steamer tying up alongside the jetty, without having said more than half a dozen sentences between them. But now Donald turned to the girl beside him.

'You are making sure, I hope, that Himself is

meeting you in London?' he said anxiously. He wasn't quite as much in awe of Sheena as his sister, and he felt his responsibility. 'It is not too late for you to be changing your plans.'

'I'll not be changing them, thank you, Donald,' said Sheena brightly, and she stepped down from the van.

'Och, then I will be bidding you goodbye, Miss Sheena,' said Donald. He deposited her little case on the ground at her feet, turned the van and drove away. He had done all he could. It was not his place to argue with Herself.

It was a beautiful day, though very windy. Carrying her case, she walked quickly along the jetty and on to the steamer. It was crammed with tourists since it was the beginning of the holiday season, and the deck was strewn with piles of hand luggage.

Sheena stood at the rail on the port side, and watched the coastline of Skye gliding past. She could see the woods of Armadale and, farther to the north, the ruins of Knock Castle on its headland. Here her ancestors had lived hundreds of years ago. No wonder Sheena's roots were in Skye!

At first the coastline was flat, but after a while it changed, and monstrous round red hills appeared to the north-west – the Red Cuillin. And now they were approaching the Narrows, where the strait between Skye and the mainland is only about a quarter of a mile wide. Over to the right were the mountains and sea lochs of Knoydart and Kintail, and when they came out of the Narrows the mountains of Apple-cross appeared like blue shadows, crowned with gleaming white. In a short time they were coming into Kyle, and she could see the ruins of Castle Maol, and behind it the round mountain called Beinn na Caillich.

By the time she reached Inverness she had only just time to catch the connection to London. As there had been no dining-car on the train from Kyle she had had nothing to eat since breakfast. The clerk at the Reservation Bureau told her cheerfully that all the standard sleeping-berths were taken.

'But I might manage to give you a first-class,' he added.

'Oh – I don't know,' faltered the girl. 'How much is it first-class?' She was thinking anxiously of the dwindling little wad of notes she had brought from home. 'I'm not sure if I can afford a first-class sleeper.'

'Och, yes, it is expensive – and of course you'll be needing a first-class ticket as well as the sleeper,' said the man. He went away, and Sheena saw him consulting a fare sheet. When he returned and told her what it would cost she drew back in dismay.

'Oh, no thank you, I won't bother,' she assured him. 'I couldn't possibly afford all that. I'll just have a single ticket to London, please. I don't really mind sitting up – at least not all that much. I suppose,' she added tentatively, 'there isn't a buffet-car on this train? Just for a cup of coffee and a sandwich.'

'No,' said the man. 'It's dinner, or nothing at all. It's a restaurant-car and not a buffet on this train.'

Eventually Sheena managed to get a cup of coffee and a packet of sandwiches from the cafeteria, and got on to the train. Although the sleeping-cars were full, there was plenty of room in the rest of the train, and Sheena found herself sharing a compartment with a fresh-faced girl hiker who had caught the sun. The two of them made themselves as comfortable as possible, one to each seat. The only trouble was that whenever the train stopped people kept opening the door, peering in and shutting it again with a loud bang, so that it was impossible to sleep.

As hour after hour passed, Sheena, looking out at the dark silent stations, began to feel depressed, and even a little frightened at what she had done. Out in the sunlight, aboard the island steamer, she had felt excited, but now, in the middle of the night, it was very different. Horrible thoughts came rushing into her mind. What if Bob Bowman was away? – she'd never thought of that! Fortunately she knew the name of Jaimie's hotel so, as a last resort, she could always go to him there. But she wanted to secure her job first. You never knew how Jaimie would take a thing. He might object to her becoming a model. In fact, the more she thought about it the more sure she became that he would! One fact stood out clearly: she must get that job quickly, for her money wouldn't last long – two days, at the most. Poor Sheena! She didn't yet know how much it costs to live in London even for so short a time as two days. She was to be sadder and wiser before many hours were over!

At last, worn out by anxiety and by her travels, she fell fast asleep, and the next thing she knew was that the girl hiker was on her feet and was hauling down an enormous rucksack that was perched on the rack above her head.

'Cheerio!' she said, hunching it on. 'King's Cross. So long!'

'Oh!' said Sheena sleepily. 'Are we here already? Why, it's still dark!'

'Six o'clock in the morning,' said the girl, opening the door. 'Nice cheerful time to arrive, I *don't* think!'

Sheena's spirits rose a little. She was actually in London. They sank again when she looked in the strip of mirror above the opposite seat. Was this – could this possibly be – lovely Sheena MacDonald? Her face looked back at her, pale and drawn. Even her hair seemed to have lost its colour, and was ruffled and untidy. She ran a comb through it, and put some powder on her nose, which made her feel better.

She wondered where she could get some breakfast so she went outside and looked about her. A great, grey, sleepy city met her eyes. It wasn't a bit like Edinburgh, which was the only big city Sheena knew, and with which she could compare London. Here were no flower gardens, no misty brown mountains, no smart shop windows draped in tartans and crammed with expensive gifts. Of course Sheena didn't know that this particular bit of London was an especially dingy bit; she just thought, Well, if this is London, I don't think much of it! I almost wish I hadn't come. If it wasn't for the modelling job . . . And that reminds me, I must find that place where Bob lives – but first I must have some breakfast. She stopped a passer-by and asked if there were any cafés open so early in the morning.

The woman, who was hurrying towards the station, slapped her on the shoulder jovially.

'Why aye, hinny!' she said in a singsong Tyneside voice. 'There's them McDonalds. Gan alang heor for aboot half a mile and ye'll find one for sure. Or mebbie yer'd rather gan i' the Undergroond.' She pointed towards the station. 'Tak' a ticket to Piccadilly Circus, and yer'll find hun'ards of cafés roond aboot there. Ta-ra, hinny!'

Poor Sheena looked after her blankly. She couldn't see any tunnel, or anything that looked like the Underground. And then suddenly she saw a red and blue sign with the name upon it. So this was the Tube she'd heard so much about! She hurried towards it, but when she had got inside and had bought her ticket the strangeness of it frightened her. The walls were covered with boards bearing strange names, and telling you how to get to the platforms, and the trains that would take you there. The one in front of her had two arrows pointing in opposite directions. 'Northbound Trains' said the one; 'Southbound Trains' said the other. But how did one know whether one wanted to go north or south? Where, for instance, was Piccadilly? She appealed to a man who was studying the board over her shoulder.

'Please, could you tell me if Piccadilly is north or south, and how do I get there?'

The man grinned.

'Ee, lass, I wish I knew!' he said in a broad Lancashire accent. 'I'm a stranger in these parts mesel', and I don't mind telling ye, I'm fair flummoxed wi' this 'ere! Why don't ee ask ticket collector? Don't look so bad for a lass! And while ye're abart it, ask 'im 'ow to get to 'Ouses o' Parliament, will ee? A'll wait for ee.'

When she came back with the information he thanked her, and went on his way. Sheena thereupon found the right platform and stood waiting for her train.

'They all goes to Piccadilly Circus that way, miss,' the ticket collector had said. 'Yer can't go wrong.' Well, she was thankful for that anyway!

The platform was almost empty at this early hour in the morning, though before very long people would be fighting and struggling to board the trains in order to get to their work. In front of the platform stretched a black length of railway track, disappearing into a dark tunnel, which, while she looked at it, was filled with sounds of fury, and out shot an infuriated train. It drew up in front of the platform with a disdainful hiss, its doors opened of their own accord and everyone got in. Never in her life had Sheena seen a train that looked as alive as this one! She stepped over the threshold of the nearest door quickly, feeling that it might snap at her and catch her in its jaws! She sat down on a seat, the doors slid closed and they were off, hurtling and racketing along through station after station, until at last PICCADILLY CIRCUS slid past the window, and Sheena knew she had arrived at her destination. Up the escalators she went and out into the chilly morning air, to find herself on one side of a big open space, with lofty buildings all around. This, then, was Piccadilly Circus, but on which side of it was the café she had come to find, or were there cafés on all the corners? There didn't seem to be one on the corner where she stood, anyway. She asked the nearest person, and this time she was lucky and was directed to a café not far away. Here she had an excellent breakfast of bacon and eggs, coffee and fresh rolls. The bill certainly gave her rather a shock, small though it would seem to a Londoner, but she felt better for the meal.

8 SHEENA FINDS BOB BOWMAN

And now, thought Sheena, for Bob Bowman. She decided to look him up straight away, since he couldn't very well be out so early in the morning. It was only – she consulted her wristwatch – why, it wasn't yet eight o'clock! She felt that it was a bit too early, perhaps, and that Bob mightn't yet be up, so she spent a little time walking round the different streets radiating from Piccadilly Circus. They all had familiar-sounding names, like Shaftesbury Avenue, Regent Street, and of course Piccadilly itself. It was beginning to rain, and her hair began to get wet – not that she minded that; she was quite used to having her hair wet, but she felt that it didn't improve her appearance. She decided, after another look at her watch, that it was time to find Bob.

Nobody seemed to have heard of the road where Bob lived, but when she said where it was they told her which buses to catch. 'It's a long way out,' volunteered one of the girls she had asked. 'Quite three miles. Take you at least an hour.'

At first Sheena thought the girl was joking. Three miles in a bus to take a whole hour. She couldn't believe it. But she soon found that in London there were so many stops and starts and traffic hold-ups that she found herself wondering how one ever got anywhere at all!

The bus driver promised to let Sheena know when to get down. 'Here y'are, miss!' he yelled at length, as the bus drew up at the corner of a dingy-looking street. 'Tooting Road.'

The bus slid away and Sheena was left standing in the road. Just beside her was Number 193, so all she had to do was to walk up this way and she'd come to Number 368b at the far end – on the other side, of course, because it was an even number.

She walked on and on. The mean street seemed endless. At Number 237 there was a long stretch of blank wall with some sort of a factory behind it, and after that an even longer stretch of iron railings. She discovered, at the far end, that the next house was only Number 239, so evidently the half-mile or so of factory and its railings only counted as one number! She went on walking. By now she had reached Number 323. Then suddenly she turned a corner and found, to her dismay, that the street seemed to have stopped for good. There was a main road here.

'But it *can't*!' said Sheena. 'Bob's number is 368, and this is only 335, so it *must* go on farther. Of course evens are on the other side, but that makes no difference.' She was to learn her mistake when she glanced across at the other side of the road. Number 2 said the house opposite, blandly and positively.

'Oh, *no*!' cried Sheena. Surely that didn't mean that the odd numbers started at one end of the street, the evens at the other?

'That's right,' said a woman to whom she appealed. 'Number 368? At the far end. Can't see it from here. Goodish way – a mile, or more.'

So back poor Sheena went. Time was moving on. It was almost twelve o'clock, and she had fears of missing Bob after all. At last she reached the other end of the long road. The houses here were even smaller and meaner. Some of them had torn and dirty lace curtains at the windows, and mangy cats sitting on the windowsills, or poking about hopefully in the overflowing dustbins. Here and there were untidy strips of garden, but in front of most of the houses was merely a plot of trampled earth. Number 368 was tidy enough anyway, thought Sheena with a sigh of relief. She was beginning by now to wish with all her heart that she hadn't come, and only the thought of the promised modelling job made her ring the bell. She stood waiting for some time, and then at last she heard a strident voice shouting inside, and the door was opened a few centimetres.

'Well?' A hard-faced woman who faintly reminded Sheena of somebody, and she realised with a shock that it was Bob, stood there staring at her through the crack in the door. 'Well?' she said again. 'What d'yer want?'

Sheena was so amazed at being spoken to like this – Herself of Glendounie was used to being treated with more respect by her fellow islanders – that she stammered, 'I – you – does Mr Bob Bowman live here?'

'And if he does,' rapped back the woman, 'what's that to you?' She didn't like the look of Sheena, with her wet auburn hair and her pale face. What had the boy been up to? This was one of his flames, no doubt. She didn't hold with her Bob getting mixed up with girls.

'I want to see Mr Bowman, please,' said Sheena, trying to muster up a little of her usual assurance.

Mrs Bowman made up her mind.

'He ain't 'ere,' she lied.

'Oh, yeah, I am, Mum,' said a voice from upstairs. 'Who's that to see me?' Bob himself bounded down the staircase, squeezed past his mother and flung open the door. When he saw Sheena he drew back. As he said afterwards to one of his mates, he was indeed struck all of a heap. He wished he'd left his mother to deal with the visitor, but now it was too late – she'd seen him!

'Er – Sheena!' he exclaimed. 'Whatever are *you* doing here?' Then, with a feeling of relief, he remembered that the dour Scotsman, for so he called Jaimie Gordon who was playing the lead in the new film whose world première was tonight, was the girl's guardian. No doubt she had come up to London with him.

'Oh, of course you've come up to town with that chap, Jaimie What's-his-name –' he began. But Sheena cut him short.

'Oh, no I haven't. Jaimie doesn't know I'm here. I thought I wouldn't tell him until I'd got the job.'

At this point Bob firmly pushed his mother, who had been gazing at Sheena all this time with her mouth open, indoors. Then he pulled the door shut and stood with Sheena outside in the rain, being careful at the same time to stand as much in the shelter of the doorway as he could.

'Job?' he echoed. 'What job?' He had a horrible suspicion.

'Why, the modelling job,' said Sheena. 'You said I had only to come – that they only had to see me and they'd jump at me. You said you had a friend –'

'See here, baby,' said Bob firmly, 'what I said to you in that benighted island was just kiddin', understand.'

'Kidding?' repeated Sheena. 'You mean –'

'I mean there ain't no job. You've got to be trained first.'

'You mean you can't just *be* a model,' said poor Sheena, 'however beautiful you are? You've got to *learn* to be one?'

'Yeah,' said Bob. 'That's right. You've got to be trained, and that costs a lot of dough.'

'How much?' persisted Sheena, not that it really mattered.

'Oh, I don't know . . . hundreds.' Bob hadn't the remotest idea how much a model's training cost. He didn't, in fact, know any models. The girl he had told Sheena about had been sheer invention. 'Now be a good kid and scoot,' he added. 'I'm busy, see.'

'And you can't help me to get *any* sort of job?' persisted the girl. 'Not on films, either?'

'Films?' Bob whistled mentally. He knew – no one better – what it took to break into films, and here was this dumbbell of a girl talking as if a film star's job was as easy to get as that of a waitress in a café! He stared at her, wondering how he had ever thought she was beautiful. Indeed, here, away from her natural surroundings, her hair disordered and streaked with rain, her face drawn with anxiety and fatigue, she looked anything but beautiful. Pitiful, some people might have thought her, but pity was a quality Bob Bowman did not possess. Some young men might have taken her in and done their best to comfort her, but Bob took after his mother. There was no softness in his nature. He was not really a very nice young man.

'Can't help you get a job of *any* sort,' he said firmly. Must get rid of the girl, he thought. He wanted to have plenty of time to dress for the film show, and goodness knows how long she'd stay if he let her in! 'I don't know why you came running after me,' he added.

This was too much for Sheena. Running after him, indeed! She'd show him!

'I regret very much to have troubled you,' she said regally and, turning on her heel, walked away, leaving Bob feeling distinctly snubbed. Oh, well – he'd got rid of her anyway, and that was the main thing. He shrugged his shoulders and went indoors, almost falling headlong over his mother, who was trying to listen through the letterbox.

'The very idea!' he said to himself, as he went upstairs. 'Taking every blessed word a chap said seriously!' While he ate his lunch he marvelled at the gullibility of Sheena. To think she thought that *he* could get jobs for her – on films, or in dressmakers showrooms – just like that! Well, that took some beating!

9 JAIMIE AND SHEENA

As Sheena walked away down the long, dreary street once more, she made up her mind. She would go to Jaimie and throw herself on his mercy. Not a very nice thought for a wilful high-spirited girl, but it was all that was left to her. He might be angry, but at least he would take care of her. She had very little money left – certainly not enough to pay for one night at a hotel. In fact, after she had paid her bus fare she had exactly three pounds left in her purse, and she still had to get to the Ruttlidge Hotel where Jaimie was staying. Oh, well – when she got there everything would be all right, she thought with a sigh of relief. If she ate humble pie Jaimie would be generous. She knew him well enough to be sure of that. She decided to blue the whole three pounds on a taxi because she didn't feel she could face the Underground again.

'Taxi!' she called, as one ambled past.

'Where to, miss?' asked the driver, as he opened the door for her.

'How much will it cost to go to the Ruttlidge

Hotel?' asked Sheena cautiously, not getting in.

'About three quid, miss,' answered the man.

'All right, but not a penny more than three pounds,' said Sheena. 'That's exactly all I have.'

'Righty-ho!' said the man. 'Jump in, miss.'

Off they sped, careering along, diving in and out of the traffic, taking short cuts known only to taxi drivers. Finally they arrived in front of the palatial entrance of the Ruttlidge Hotel. It must be explained that Jaimie was not staying at the Ruttlidge because of the rise in his financial situation, but merely because the YMCA hostel happened to be full! Out came a splendid commissionaire, covered in gold braid, who flung open the taxi door and drew back a little when he beheld a white-faced, wet girl, with no luggage to speak of.

The taxi driver stood looking from the money which Sheena had counted into his hand to the girl. So she'd been speaking the truth! It was all she had. Her last three quid!

'Too much,' he said firmly, handing her back one pound. Couldn't take her last pound! 'Come quicker than I thought. Good luck, miss!'

'Are you staying at the hotel, madam?' asked the commissionaire. He didn't suppose she was, but one had to be careful.

'Yes – I mean no – not exactly,' faltered Sheena. Her assurance vanished before his splendour; she felt indeed a stranger in a strange land. 'A – a friend of mine is staying here. His name is Gordon – Jaimie Gordon.'

'Mr Gordon?' repeated the man. 'Do you know the number of his room, madam?'

She shook her head.

'If you'll come inside, madam, we'll soon find out,' said the commissionaire. He took her arm and led her into the vestibule. Heads turned to follow them. Had the girl been caught doing something she shouldn't? You could almost hear the sigh of disappointment when the man led the girl over the thickly carpeted vestibule to the reception desk and handed her over to the receptionist. It didn't take long to find out that Jaimie's room was Number 147, and all that now remained was to contact him.

'We'll page him,' said the receptionist. 'If you'll just take a seat . . . '

Sheena took a seat thankfully – her knees were beginning to feel weak.

'Will Mr Gordon, room number 147, please come to Reception . . . Will Mr Gordon, room number 147, please come . . . ' Sheena sat listening to the slightly supercilious voice of the receptionist paging for Jaimie. 'Will Mr Gordon . . . '

But no Mr Gordon appeared at Reception, and finally the receptionist beckoned to Sheena.

'I'm afraid Mr Gordon is not in the hotel at the moment, madam,' she said. 'Perhaps you could call back later.'

It was, by now, nearly teatime, so Sheena went into a snack bar and spent her remaining money on a cup of tea and a bun. The very thought of braving the Ruttlidge Hotel again made her turn pale, but it had to be done. Somehow, some time, she must contact Jaimie.

It was nearly six o'clock when she finally screwed up enough courage to walk once more through the swing doors of the great hotel and approach the reception desk.

The receptionist looked her up and down superciliously. 'Can I help you, madam?'

'My friend – Mr Gordon – is he in yet?' asked Sheena. 'You remember – you told me to come back . . .'

'Oh, that must have been Cecile,' said the receptionist. 'I've just come on duty, you see. Mr Gordon, you say? Shall I page him for you?'

'If it's the gent in Number 147, it ain't no use paging '*im*,' put in an hotel porter, glittering with gold buttons. ''E's out. I seed 'im go. A real 'Ighlander, kilt an' all! And the other gent, too. All togged up, the two of 'em, fit to kill, ready for the film premiére. Some folk 'ave all the luck!'

'The film première?' questioned Sheena.

'That's right, madam, *Pride o' the North* its name is. Première at the Unicorn Theatre, in the Strand. They say royalty's to be there. I'd like to bet them two gents gets presented.'

'Then you mean he won't be back till late tonight?' said Sheena with sinking heart.

'Shouldn't think so, madam,' said the porter brightly. 'Heared him tellin' the other gent they was to get dinner out afore the show, and supper after. Shouldn't think they'll be back here till early tomorrer mornin'.'

Suddenly it dawned upon Sheena what Jaimie had done. He had received an invitation to the first showing of his film and told her not a word of it. Perfidious, treacherous Jaimie! And she had thought he loved her! Well, she knew better now. Probably he was taking another girl to the première!

She turned and almost ran out of the hotel, scarcely heeding the curious glances that were cast in her direction.

Sheena was now in a pretty plight. She literally hadn't a penny and, apart from Jaimie – and Annette, whose address she didn't know – she hadn't a single soul to turn to in all this great city. Not a very nice thought, with night coming on! She decided there was only one thing to do. She must just walk about until the film show was over and then go back to the hotel, no matter how late the hour. Whatever Jaimie had done, and however little he thought of her, he was still her guardian. 'And goodness knows,' said poor Sheena, 'what he will think of me, turning up at his hotel in the early hours of the morning! I am thinking he will be very shocked.'

London, let it be said, is the easiest place in the world to pass away the time in, always provided you have plenty of money in your pocket; but it is also the hardest if you are stony-broke. The girl wandered up this street and down that one, into a wide square filled with fluttering pigeons, and stood looking up at a mighty column on the top of which was a figure with a cocked hat.

Lord Nelson, thought Sheena. Well, I can always say I've seen him!

It had begun to rain again – cold, penetrating rain that wet her through and through. Not that she minded, really – it made London seem more like home to her! She wandered down a flight of steps and found herself looking over a parapet into a murky river. All along its banks were tall buildings, glittering like palaces, and reflecting in the water. She walked across a bridge and looked back. Some of the buildings looked vaguely familiar. She realised with a shock of surprise that she was looking across at the Houses of Parliament!

Sheena stayed down by the river for a very long time. There is something friendly about the Embankment that attracts the unfortunate and those who have nowhere to go. For one thing, there are seats where they can rest their tired feet! It was eleven o'clock when she eventually climbed wearily up one of the steep streets into the Strand. Above one of the buildings was a neon sign – a unicorn, traced out in flashing lights, and above it names in glowing red letters, but she was too near to read them. Just as Sheena arrived a car drove away and a cheer went up from the waiting crowd.

'It's her!' said one of the onlookers, turning to Sheena. 'Looked lovely, didn't she, in that silver dress and those sapphires, but then she always does, bless her! Wonder how much that jewellery cost? Pretty penny, I'd like to guess! Bet some of them folk in there –' he nodded at the glass doors through which could be seen a dazzling crowd of people milling about '– are rolling in it too! Look at that one, now – pretty, ain't she? Bet she's a film star!' A girl in an oyster satin dress, closely fitting to her slender figure, had appeared near the doors.

'Why, it's Annette!' cried Sheena. 'Annette Dancy!'

The figure turned half round and another joined it – a kilted figure, with curly black hair and dark eyes. The two began to talk to each other and, as she watched them, a stab of jealousy shot through Sheena's heart. Jaimie and Annette Dancy! So *that*'s how it was! *That*'s why she hadn't been told about the film première!

Oh, how miserable I am, thought Sheena, and she turned once more and stumbled out of the crowd.

But even as she did so, the young Highlander glanced through the doors and saw her. Not for nothing were his eyes trained to see things that no ordinary person's would have noticed. In a flash he had swung open the doors, had dived into the crowd and caught Sheena by the arm, to the electrification of the crowd, who imagined it must all be part of the film première! He did not ask her why she was there.

Enough for him to know that she was wet and cold and in need of comfort. Up to the present he had merely thought she was beautiful and wild, and had sometimes had a swift desire to tame her, but now, as he looked down at her pale tired face, a feeling of tenderness for her came into his heart for the first time. Moreover she was his ward, and very young and foolish. He must take care of her. He spoke to her in the Gaelic, so we shall never know what he said, any more than the fascinated crowd did.

'We will go now to my hotel,' he said at length in English. 'We must be getting a room for you.' Notice that he no longer thought about convention. It was more important to get his young ward warm and comfortable. 'And then, after we have done so, and after you have eaten, we will be talking about this matter, and you will be telling me how it is you came to do so foolish a thing.'

Sheena, clinging to his arm, nodded silently, knowing that if she spoke she would burst into tears, and this would never do in front of a London crowd! A faint ray of comfort warmed her sore heart. Although Jaimie was going to scold her, he obviously thought more about her comfort than about the glittering company of people in the theatre – yes, even including Annette Dancy, thought Sheena jealously!

10 THE FILM PREMIÈRE

Dressing for the film show had been the most exciting part of it all, thought Annette. Paddy and Marie had both come to the convent home to help, and Annette's little room soon began to look like a beauty salon. Even the nuns smiled indulgently when they passed the bathroom, out of which came whiffs of the most enchanting perfume, for of course, as Marie said, one must smell as nice as one looks.

Annette was made to promise that she wouldn't as much as glance in a full-length mirror until she was quite finished, and as a matter of fact this was a very easy promise to keep since the one and only full-length mirror in the whole convent home happened to be on the ground floor in the room of an elderly spinster called Miss Murchison. The room had once belonged to a girl who was studying to be a dress designer at an art school, and she had had a strip of mirror fixed to the back of the door, and there it had remained ever since, so that the occupant of the room was the envy of the whole convent home. If anyone was going out for the evening, she always popped in to pay Miss Murchison a visit and look in her mirror! It need hardly be said that Miss Murchison was one of the most popular people in the home!

To be sure, Annette, like everyone else, had a small square of looking-glass perched above her chest of drawers, but unless you tilted it at a certain angle it was impossible to see the whole of your face at once. Not that it mattered much upon ordinary occasions because Annette didn't bother a great deal about her face, other than removing stage make-up with cleansing cream and washing it with soap and water. To Paddy and Marie's horror she confessed that she didn't possess any everyday make-up at all – not even a lipstick. So Marie had generously brought along her own beauty-box and put it at Annette's disposal, and between them she and Paddy made such a transformation that, as Paddy said, 'Sure, an' your own mother wouldn't know you, Annette Dancy!' There was a lot of truth in this statement, for Mrs Dancy would indeed have had a job to recognise in the elegant young lady, wearing the French model gown, her own tousle-headed, untidy daughter!

There was a very special reason for the care that Paddy and Marie were taking over Annette's appearance – besides the film show. She had been chosen to present a bouquet of roses and carnations to royalty. After all, who more suitable than a little dancer, they all said. She would at least be able to curtsy gracefully!

At length the three girls pattered down the many flights of stairs to Miss Murchison's room, and many were the compliments Annette received from the people they met on the way, not to mention the even more complimentary fact that some of them didn't recognise her! When she stood at last in front of the long mirror, she said nothing at all for quite a minute. She just couldn't believe that this beautifully groomed and dressed girl was really Annette Dancy. Of course she was used to seeing herself beautifully dressed in ballet clothes, but this was different. Facing her in the mirror was a stately young lady wearing a long evening dress of gleaming satin, folded and draped to her slender figure and falling in a little train behind. The bodice and the train were embroidered in pearls and sequins, and glittered softly when she moved or breathed. Her hair shone like a raven's wing, due to much brushing on the part of the little French hairdresser. Her elbow-length gloves were softly wrinkled on her slender arms, and her silver slippers just peeped out from the front of her dress as she walked. It was strange, unbelievable! Why, she was almost beautiful!

'Thank you, thank you, Marie – both of you!' she said, turning to them with shining eyes.

'*Enchanté!*' said Marie. 'Eet 'as been *un plaisir, ma chère*.'

'A pleasure, so it has!' echoed Paddy. 'It's time for you to go, Annette, mavourneen. You must not keep the young men waiting too long.' Annette was having dinner with Jaimie and Angus before the show. 'Here is your cloak and your bag.'

Wrapped in the velvet cloak, with Marie holding up her train, and half the convent home looking out of the windows, Annette stepped into the taxi that Paddy had summoned and away she went. Her two friends were following later on, for since they had been in the film ballet, they had also got tickets.

When Annette was asked afterwards about the film première, and what it felt like being presented to royalty, she hadn't much to say. There was a special word said to Meriel, who had so nearly lost her life while making this film, and also to Jaimie and Angus, who had rescued her at risk of their own. Also to little Annette, who had danced so charmingly, and who was now presenting these beautiful flowers . . .

In a very short time royalty had passed into the theatre, where a royal box had been specially made in the centre of the grand circle. Annette noticed how carefully the flowers were laid on the ledge in front of her, as if they were a very first bouquet. She looks a little lonely, thought Annette, as she watched the slim figure, seated all by herself in her glittering white dress. No matter how tired she feels, or how sad, and she must often feel both, thought Annette, royalty must always be gracious, always thank with smiles, and listen gravely to whatever is being said. No, it was certainly no easy job being royal! One must not even yawn when bored!

Then Annette forgot about everything else, for the lights had gone down and the film had begun. It was strange to see Jaimie's name, and her own, in big letters at the beginning, and even stranger to see Jaimie himself, walking about and talking exactly as he did in real life. He didn't seem to be acting at all! And then there was herself, dancing! She hadn't seen

the rushes of the ballet sequences, and now, watching them for the first time, she couldn't help feeling a thrill of pride. Here was *La Sylphide* danced the way it should be, the way Bournonville, the Danish choreographer, had meant it to be danced. Then came the scenes in Skye. Oh, how lovely it was to see Airdrochan Castle again, and the loch, and Blaven, looking terrifyingly big and rugged, with the sun setting behind the jagged ridge of Clach Glas! After this came the scene in Coire Lagan, with the awful stone shoot, filled with boiling mist and the noise of falling scree, and then the dramatic rescue on the Inaccessible Pinnacle. Annette had not seen any of this before, and shivers of sheer terror ran up and down her spine as she watched the tiny figures negotiating the huge crack in the rocky peak. As for the accident – she knew, of course, that it was real, for Angus had told her all about it in a letter – she had to shut her eyes, and clench her hands to stop herself from screaming!

And then it was all over, and they were all coming out of the theatre, and Annette was meeting her friends in the vestibule downstairs.

'Oh, hello, Jaimie!' she cried. 'I thought you were quite splendid! But oh – isn't it hot! Let's go to the door and get a breath of fresh air.'

But when they got to the door they dare not open it because of the crush of people outside who, having seen royalty depart, were waiting patiently to see some of the film stars. However, it was certainly cooler over here, so they stood for a while looking at the huge crowd outside. And then Angus came up, and he had to tell Annette how lovely he thought her dancing, and she had to tell him how wonderful she had thought his part in the film.

'I wasn't meant to have any part in it at all, you know,' he laughed. 'I was just an extra roped in for a few metres of climbing, if you'll excuse the pun! Good lord! – What is Jaimie doing?' The young Highlander had suddenly flung open the glass doors and vanished into the crowd, for no reason at all – or at least no reason as far as they could see. We know better!

'Well!' said Annette in astonishment. 'And he was just telling me it would be unwise – you know his old-fashioned way of speaking – to go out there while the crowd's so big. Would you believe it?'

'There will be a reason,' said Angus, who knew Jaimie better than Annette did.

Just at this moment something happened that drove all thoughts of Jaimie, or indeed anything else, completely out of Annette's mind. Mr Goldberg appeared, and by his side was a dark little man in immaculate evening dress. Even Annette couldn't help noticing how beautiful it was, and also the black pearls in his shirt front. He had expressive hands, which he used a great deal as he talked, and on which glittered more than one diamond ring. His features were fine, though a little cruel, she thought, and his nose slightly hooked. Although he spoke with a slight accent of some sort and bowed from the waist, she didn't think he was a foreigner.

'Annette,' said Stanley Goldberg, 'I want to introduce –' he made a dramatic pause ' – Mr Solomon Isaacs.'

Annette gasped. Mr Solomon Isaacs, the world-famous film producer! She'd heard of him, of course – everybody had!

'Mr Isaacs wants to tempt you to go to Hollywood,' Stanley Goldberg was saying, just as if it were the most ordinary thing in the world.

'To – to – *Hollywood*!' gasped Annette.

'Listen to me,' commanded Mr Isaacs, as though he were more used to people listening to him than he was to listening to other people. He proceeded to paint for Annette a glowing picture of her life should she allow him to sign her up for his next picture – the fame that would be hers, the adulation she would receive, the money she would be paid.

'But I'm not a film actress. I'm a dancer,' protested Annette to no avail, for Mr Isaacs didn't take the slightest notice.

'My dear young lady, do you imagine I have not been watching you?' he exclaimed. 'All this evening I have watched you. I have not looked at anyone else! Your face has as many expressions on it in one hour as most people in one year!' He threw up his hands in an expressive gesture. 'Stanley, old fox, to produce a girl who can not only dance like Fonteyn but act as well! Where did you find her?'

'You must not say that!' ordered Annette, her eyes flashing.

'Must not say what, my dear?'

'That about Fonteyn. It's not true. I don't dance like Fonteyn, because no one does. Besides, I don't *want* to dance like Fonteyn, however wonderful she was. I want to dance like *myself*.'

'Of course, of course!' murmured Mr Isaacs soothingly. 'But let us talk about my film, shall we? It is called *The Fallen Star*, and it is about a dancer who has fallen on evil days.'

'Oh, what happened to her?' asked Annette with a gleam of interest.

Mr Isaacs shrugged his shoulders.

'Does that matter? Enough to say that she cannot

dance for some reason or other, and then she makes a comeback. This would be a wonderful part for you, would it not?'

'I don't know,' said Annette candidly. 'I should have to know a lot more about it. It sounds rather silly so far.'

Mr Isaacs skated over the thin ice of the film plot, and remarked casually, 'Your salary would be substantial.' He named a figure.

Annette's head swam. She didn't want to act in films; she wanted to dance. But here was temptation! It wasn't for herself she wanted the money but for her mother. All her mother's difficulties could be at an end if she made this one film. It was Jaimie all over again!

'Oh, but I'm not sure that I could go to Hollywood anyway,' she said cautiously. 'I'm not very old, you know. I'm only sixteen. I couldn't go to America all by myself, could I?'

Mr Isaacs didn't say that lots of girls *have* gone to Hollywood at that age, or that he knew hundreds who would go to Timbuktu, or the African jungle, or the North Pole if the salary was high enough. He said soothingly, 'Your mother could come with you. You have a mother, have you not? Good! Your two flights would be paid – first-class of course.'

'Oh!' said Annette, not knowing whether to feel pleased or sorry. All her difficulties were being removed by this persistent man. How her mother would love it! What a change it would be for her! No chores of any sort! And, above all, lots of lovely clothes to wear. Her mother hardly ever had a new dress, thought Annette sadly.

'I – I'll think about it,' she promised.

'Thank you, my dear,' said Mr Isaacs with a bow. 'This weekend I shall contact you again, and we will have the contract all drawn up and ready for you to sign. *Au revoir*, my dear.' He bowed again in stately fashion and was gone, leaving Annette looking after him, her thoughts in a whirl.

That night Annette rang up her mother. But she didn't have very long to discuss something that was going to change her whole life!

'You'll love going to America, won't you, Mummy?' she said anxiously, after she had told her mother the world-shattering news.

And 'Of course I shall love it, darling,' bravely lied Mrs Dancy at the other end of the line, for she felt she couldn't stand in Annette's way now she had got this wonderful opportunity. The child's fortune was made, it appeared, and although it seemed strange to her to think that Annette was going to make films instead of dancing in ballets, it wasn't her place to say so. She'd always believed in letting her children manage their own lives. One thing was quite certain, however, and that was that Annette would never make very much money dancing in any ballet company.

'Of course I'll come to America with you, if that

will make you happy,' repeated poor Mrs Dancy, appalled and terrified at the mere thought of it.

'First-class, Mummy,' said Annette into the telephone. 'Mr Isaacs promised we would travel first-class. And you'll be able to dress for dinner every night, and wear lovely clothes, and have glorious meals, and see all the places you've always said you wanted to see . . . ' She talked on and on, while Mrs Dancy, at the other end, thought how very different it was saying one wanted to see distant lands from actually going there, when it came to the point!

And then Annette had to say goodbye. Mrs Dancy, three hundred miles away in distant Northumberland, sighed as she put down the receiver.

'Why the sigh, my dear?' said Mr MacCrimmon, the vicar, coming into the room.

'I've just had some news,' said Mrs Dancy. 'And I don't know what to feel about it. Annette's going to Hollywood, and I am afraid I shall have to go with her.'

11 THE LITTLE DANCER

All the next week Annette thought about her future, and the more she thought the gloomier she grew! For one thing, she had had a stormy interview with Monsieur Georges. He hadn't minced matters. He had called her a gold-digger.

'Oh, but I'm not – really I'm not,' protested Annette. 'If it were only for myself – but you see, there's Mummy.'

Monsieur Georges shrugged his shoulders. He had seen plenty of these gold-digging mamas.

'Ah, these mothers!' he exclaimed in a fury. 'They will sell their souls – or their daughters – for a few American dollars!'

'Oh, no, you're quite wrong,' cried Annette in distress. 'Mummy's not a bit like that. But you see, she's a clergyman's widow, and you know what the clergy are – they simply haven't got a penny. Mummy can only live in half the vicarage, as it is, and if it wasn't for the hens she couldn't live at all. But if I went to Hollywood and made just this one film, all the money I made could be invested and my mother would be able to live on the interest all her life. That's what Jaimie did, you know, so I can't think it's wrong. And I know,' she added, 'that poor Mummy sometimes feels afraid for the future, because I've seen her looking so sad. It's not nice to be poor when you're young, but when you're old it's ever so much worse, and Mummy's at least forty-five.' By this time Annette was nearly in tears herself at her impassioned appeal. 'So if I made just this one film –'

'They all say that,' declared Monsieur Georges, unmoved. 'You say it yourself a short while ago. You come to me and you say, "Maestro, I weesh to be in zis film *Pride o' the North*, or whatever its so stupid name is. On-ly zis one film," you say, "and after that I weel work. 'Ow I weel work!" And now see what

'appen! Eet ees ze small end of ze wedge! If you go to 'Ollywood you weel nevaire return – nevaire, nevaire, you understand?'

'Oh, but I *should*,' cried Annette.

Monsieur Georges shrugged again.

'So they all say! And when do you go, if one may be permitted to ask?'

'I don't know yet,' she answered, 'Mr Isaacs hasn't said, but I expect it won't be for ages and ages.'

She rang up Mr Isaacs that night and told him that she had decided to sign the contract. Although, of course, she couldn't see him, she could feel him rubbing his hands.

'That is good,' he said. 'Very good. You are a wise little girl, and I promise that you will not regret it, my dear. I will make arrangements for the contract to be ready for you to sign at your solicitors on Saturday. I understand that they are Brown and Ingless, of Duke Street?'

'And Mummy is to come with me?' said Annette. 'First-class. You promised?'

'Certainly,' said Mr Isaacs affably, thinking to himself, And cheap at the price! We can put up with the mother for the time being, and get rid of her afterwards. The main thing is to secure the child. 'By the way,' he added aloud, 'we fly in a week's time. I shall see to all the bookings.'

'A week's time!' cried Annette in dismay. 'Oh, I didn't think it would be as soon as that.'

'Time is money in the film industry,' said the

producer, ringing off quickly. Nothing like the telephone to curtail arguments! And incidentally, by so doing, he lost Annette!

And now Annette was sadder than ever, for on the day of the competition for the Cecchetti Casket she would be in America, and someone else would be dancing her role of the Little Matchgirl – the role she had dreamed of for so long. Someone else would win the Casket for the Georges Reinholt ballet-school. Oh, she couldn't think about it without crying! If only, if only it wasn't for her darling mother!

All Friday she wandered about like a sad little ghost. For one thing, she had nothing to do. It was no use going back to the ballet-school for the term was finished, and she couldn't bear to watch them rehearsing *The Little Matchgirl*. Paddy or Marie would be taking her place, she supposed, for she had rung up Monsieur Georges and told him the date she was due to leave. She hadn't dared to see him personally.

She bought one or two things that she would need and made a list of the things she wanted to pack and those she would leave behind. Strange to think that her mother would be doing the same thing up in Northumberland!

In the late afternoon she walked up the Embankment, trying to think about the excitement ahead – the places she would see. How her mother would adore travelling for the first time in her life! She'd never had enough money even to cross the Channel to Ostend. They'd often laughed about it, and Mrs Dancy had said she'd probably live and die without ever having been outside the British Isles. She wouldn't be able to say that now! As for Annette herself, she had all the luck! Most girls would give their eyes to be Annette Dancy, with a film contract in her pocket, at least, it would be in her pocket at this time tomorrow, and a glittering future ahead of her. If only – if only she wasn't haunted by the thought of Monsieur Georges's ballet, and the coveted role that had been hers for so short a time, the role that would now be danced by Paddy or Marie. If only they had been leaving a week later! She was haunted by the thought of the ballet company too. They would all be in it together and only she would be missing.

'Oh, happy, happy Annette Dancy!' cried Annette, the tears rolling down her cheeks.

She found herself outside the Tate Gallery, and almost without knowing it she walked up the steps and into the vestibule. It was peaceful in there, and there was something about it that made her feel less lonely. She wandered into one gallery after another, and came at length to the collection of Dégas bronzes, the most famous one of all, standing by itself in a glass case, in the centre of the gallery. It was the figure of a little girl with thin legs, and hands clasped behind her back. She wore a real net ballet-dress, thin and dark with age, and her hair was tied

back with a real bit of faded yellow ribbon.

'Oh, it's *La Petite Danseuse*!' cried Annette. 'The Little Dancer.' She stood in front of the glass case, hands behind her back, unconsciously copying the attitude of the famous bronze, and standing there looking at it, she forgot her troubles. Dégas' dancer was ugly but there was something strangely fascinating about her – you might perhaps call it single-mindedness. There she stood, gazing down the gallery as she would gaze down the centuries, seeing nothing but her own dreams, typifying all the hundreds of little dancers, of all countries, and all schools, past and to come. And Annette Dancy was one of them!

'Oh, I know it now!' cried Annette so loudly that several people turned round and stared at her. 'I can't go to Hollywood. I must ring Mummy up straight away and tell her I'm so sorry, but I can't go. You see I'm not a film star at all. I'm just like *her*,' she nodded to the little statue. 'I'm a little dancer!'

Turning, she ran out of the gallery towards the nearest telephone box . . .